PERSONAL WAR
PART 3

by

Dave Aquino

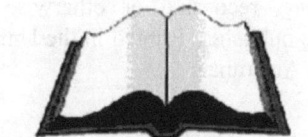

CCB Publishing
British Columbia, Canada

Personal War Part 3

Copyright ©2014 by Dave Aquino
ISBN-13   978-1-77143-157-6
First Edition

Library and Archives Canada Cataloguing in Publication
Aquino, Dave, 1981-, author
Personal war part 3 / by Dave Aquino. -- First edition.
Issued in print and electronic formats.
ISBN 978-1-77143-157-6 (pbk.).--ISBN 978-1-77143-158-3 (pdf)
Additional cataloguing data available from Library and Archives Canada

Cover artwork credit: Man facing mirror © henkstolk | Canstockphoto.com
Vintage round wall clock © Alexandre17 | Canstockphoto.com
Broken glass with cracks © buch | Canstockphoto.com

This is a work of fiction. Names, places, and characters are a product of the author's imagination or are used fictitiously and are not to be considered as real. Resemblance to any events or persons, living or dead, past or present, is purely coincidental.

Extreme care has been taken by the author to ensure that all information presented in this book is accurate and up to date at the time of publishing. Neither the author nor the publisher can be held responsible for any errors or omissions. Additionally, neither is any liability assumed for damages resulting from the use of the information contained herein.

Publisher: CCB Publishing
             British Columbia, Canada
             www.ccbpublishing.com

Contents

Contents

Chapter 1

Party in the County Jail

Riley Rosagalio stood alone on the steps of a large, old, brick building downtown. A tall, thin man, he cut a sharp figure in his tailored navy blue suit. The light summer breeze ruffled his short black hair as he paced back and forth. Every few steps he adjusted his silver wire frame glasses and peered up the street.

All around him birds sang in the branches of lush green trees that reached up against a cloudless blue sky. Children raced up and down the street on their bicycles while the old folks sat on their porches talking and listening to the ball game on the radio. Just another early summer afternoon in Small Town, U.S.A.

All nice and normal, Riley thought. Then he looked up at the building in front of him. Well, not exactly normal, he corrected. At least he hoped that calls like the one that had brought him down here weren't going to become normal. He didn't think he could go through that again.

Up the block a short, slightly pudgy man with curly brown hair came around the corner. Though it was warm, he wore a black windbreaker over his sea green hospital scrubs. Riley waved. The man, Mitch, Riley's best friend since high school, waved back. Mitch jogged the half block separating them and then stood on the steps wheezing as he tried to catch his breath.

"Took you long enough," said Riley.

"Had to find someone to cover my shift," Mitch said between coughs. "Bedpans don't empty themselves."

"Yeah. Restaurants don't run themselves, either." Riley looked up at the building again.

"How bad can it be?" Mitch asked.

"Well it can't be good. We're visiting him in jail," Riley replied.

"Yeah, but it's only the city lockup."

"That doesn't always mean anything, maybe the county was full."

"Let's just see what's up."

Both of them took a deep breath and entered the large brick building. The door slammed behind them, instantly cutting off the beautiful day outside. A chill swept over the two men as the last of the sun's warmth on their skin was blown away by a cold blast of machine circulated air. Riley wrinkled his nose as the smells of dust, mildew and burnt coffee hit his nostrils. Beside him Mitch coughed quietly.

A thick paper collage of wanted posters, police bulletins and crime prevention tips covered most of the space on the dingy gray walls, broken only by the placement of a few narrow, barred windows. The dim florescent lights reflected dully on the filthy glass. A long brown Formica counter ran the length of the room, it's top and front scarred by years of being kicked, slapped, leaned on and abused in other ways.

Behind the counter a short, heavy-set sheriff's deputy with thinning blond hair stood chewing on the end of his thick mustache. He glared at Mitch and Riley as they slowly made their way across the cracked linoleum floor.

"You guys here to visit a convict?" asked the cop.

"Um, I don't believe he's been convicted of anything," said Riley.

"Yeah, yeah. 'Innocent until proven guilty' and all that crap. Everybody's innocent. Nobody's ever guilty of nothin'. The crimes commit themselves and good old lyin' lawyers smear good cops to stand up for the rights of the victims we mistakenly call suspects. Oops, excuse me, 'persons of interest'. We can't call them suspects anymore or we get sued, even if we know damn well they did it. God bless America, home of the crook."

Riley and Mitch exchanged stunned looks. Riley's mouth opened and closed several times as he tried to phrase a response, but nothing came to mind.

"Gimme your I.D.s," the cop barked.

Mitch and Riley hurried to comply. The cop shook his head and walked towards a computer at the back of the room. He spent almost

20 minutes running their names through various background checks and criminal databases before returning to the counter.

"Well looks like we haven't caught you two yet," he said, throwing their I.D.s back at them.

"Excuse me, sir" said Mitch. "What makes you so sure we're criminals?"

"Well, you're here to visit one."

"Huh?"

"Well, I'm just sayin', 'thugs of a feather' and all that. Usually the only people who visit an inmate are his fellow gangbangers."

"Do we look like gangbangers to you?" asked Riley.

The cop looked him up and down. "Actually, you kinda look like the two bit divorce lawyer that took my cousin Marty to the cleaners. Talk about a criminal! Speaking of, which of our distinguished guests are you fellas here to visit this afternoon?"

"We'd like to see William Defreno, please," Riley said in a strained voice.

The cop grinned. "Well, why didn't you say so! Right this way, gentlemen."

The cop opened a little door at the side of the counter and stood aside to let them through. He led Riley and Mitch through a hallway towards the back of the building. Riley started to turn left towards the cell block, but the officer stopped him.

"Where you goin'?" the cop asked.

"Uh..." Riley pointed to the sign above a doorway that said "Visiting Room".

"Oh no, not in there. Mr. Defreno will see you in the conference room." Riley's eyebrows shot up. Mr. Defreno? Conference room??

The officer led them into a room about 20 feet further along the hall.

"Can I get you gentlemen anything while you wait? Coffee? Soft drink? Maybe a fresh pastry? "

"I think we're good, thanks," said Riley. All of this was starting to feel a bit too surreal.

"Alright. Make yourselves comfortable. Mr. Defreno will be with you shortly."

As the door closed, Riley turned to Mitch.

"You ever heard of a jail serving refreshments and letting a prisoner use the conference room for his private visits?"

"I've never heard of a jail having a conference room," replied Mitch. "I thought we'd been visiting through glass with the little phone thingy- you know like on T.V.?"

"Yeah, me too."

Both of them waited as good naturedly as they could. It was hard because they really wanted to talk to William now and see just how bad of a nightmare this episode was going be.

William came in escorted by a deputy. Though he wore the jail's standard orange jump suit, there were no cuffs or chains anywhere on him. He came in drinking a soda and thanked the deputy for asking if he needed anything. Mitch and Riley looked at each other mystified. A closer look revealed a black eye and red soreness on his face.

"Mitch, Riley, what did I miss?" William said as he put his hands together to make a loud clap noise that echoed in the room. The noise irritated Riley who was already on his last nerve.

"Wow that was a loud clap," Mitch laughed. "Look at Riley, he's really pissed off now."

William nodded his head with a dumb look on his face as he approached the two of them.

"Glad to see ya." He continued seeming overly cheerful for someone beat up and in an orange jump suit. Riley couldn't decide what to do or think. Was he acting like this to try to cover up the fact that he was back in jail after so many clean years? If that was the case he didn't want to crash his good cocky mood with hard reality. Also, it was possible William had lost his mind again and this visit would just be a bunch of senseless gibberish.

"Uh," Riley started. "I was gonna ask you the same question. What am I missing?"

"What?"

"How's the food here? Is it as good as the food at the hospital?" Mitch interjected.

"Man, the cook here is the shit, I mean we gotta get this guy to the diner. Whatever they're payin' him I'll double it."

"Never mind the food," Riley yelled. "Just shut up! What the hell is going on?"

"I can't tell you what happened."

"Why?" Riley demanded.

"You told me to shut up."

Mitch laughed as Riley rolled his eyes.

"Okay wise guy, I'm outta here. Come on, Mitch, let's go enjoy the fresh air and sunshine," Riley said.

"This is nothing!" William yelled. "I got caught fighting in public with that little, that little son of a bitch, whatever the punk's name is."

"You mean that Roger Delahoy kid?" Riley asked as he sat back down.

"Yeah, that's the one. At least they won't try to give me fourteen years for it."

"Probably not."

"Remember when I was arrested for doing nothing, cause the Casners bribed the cops to arrest me? I was gonna get fourteen years."

"Yes, I remember it well, plus you mention it all the time," Riley answered.

"You know, if I had gotten fourteen years back then I'd be getting out this year."

"William," Riley said as he put his face in his hand. "We are kicking ass! I mean in less than a year Moe's Diner went from a little hole in the wall to corporate restaurants taking a hit from all the business in town we get. Lois sold it to you at a good price and now it's actually making real money."

"Yeah. I know."

"Well, I wanna know why you are risking losing the business for doing dumb things like fighting."

"No, you don't."

"No! I wanna know why!" Riley barked out.

"Oh God! Yer just gonna laugh or tell me I'm fucking up again. Let's talk about something else. Did your mom get her new house?"

"Yes. She bought the one in the Paradise Cottage neighborhood."

"Oh, is that what that neighborhood in named now?" William asked with a sneer.

"Um, isn't that was it always called?" Riley said with one big eye as he realized he would regret asking, but thought it was too late to take it back. He didn't know what this latest tangent of William's was all he knew was it would be more garbage conversation.

"What was it called, William?" Mitch asked, excited. "I always thought it was called Paradise Cottages."

"Nope, when Randy Casner owned the town that neighborhood was called 'Ranin-grad' it was a prize neighborhood for him."

Mitch laughed at the bizarre reference to Leningrad and the underlying punch-line that Randy had been like a Russian dictator in their home town. Riley was already stale about William's Randy Casner jokes in general, but was fuming even more now because this was not the time or place for such stupid humor. He decided to let Mitch and William have their laugh at the stupid reference, but they hooted about it for too long.

"Well," Riley said as he thumped his fist on the table. "Sorry to be the bearer of bad news, but you're in jail again. You haven't been arrested for almost ten years since the Timmy thing."

"I know and you're right. You've always been right. Even in high school you were always right. But you were always too damn late."

"Well, maybe you'll listen to me now."

"Too late, too late." William replied in an eccentric tone.

"What happened? Tell me now or I'm going home."

"I don't think you'll actually leave," a cocky William said. Riley gave William the one big eye look and put both hands on the table as if he was ready to get up and leave. Whatever it was making him act this way it was clear that Riley may not be bluffing. William cleared his throat and surrendered his goofy mood to Riley's threat.

"Oh all right, It started the day I let Lois come back and see what I'd done to the Diner."

Two days before:

Lois and William stood on the new brick walkway outside of Moe's Diner.

"Are you ready for this?" William asked.

Lois took a deep breath and smiled. "You bet. Can't wait to see what you've done with the place."

"Well, the first thing you should know is that I now have these people called customers who come here now."

"Wise ass," said Lois. "If you have customers where are they all?"

"We close for two hours in the afternoon. It gives us time to reset for dinner service and run errands."

"Don't you lose money closing in the middle of the day?"

"We more than make up for it by having time to prep more high end dishes for the dinner crowd."

Lois shook her head. "I never really thought of Moe's as 'high end'."

"Well, it is now." William pushed open one side of the glass double doors. "After you."

Lois paused to inspect the door frame. "These are new," she said.

"Yep. No more bent hinges. They actually close without snagging the carpet. The lock doesn't jam anymore, either."

"Nice."

"Oh, this is just the beginning," said William.

They walked into the dining room. Lois's mouth dropped in shock. The clean, bright space was completely unrecognizable.

"Oh, William!" said Lois.

"You like it?"

"It's unbelievable!"

A new dark wood lunch counter with a white granite top had been installed to the left of the front doors. A sleek new modern cash register and computerized order pad sat at the end of the counter facing the door. A large dessert case sat at the other end. Under the glass, rich looking pies and soft, puffy cakes glistened invitingly. Behind the counter, prints of classic movie posters in black frames with red mats hung on the bright white plaster wall. Red leather low-backed stools swiveled on chrome posts set in the floor along the counter's front.

"Not your average diner stool," said Lois.

"Not your average diner," said William. He handed her a menu in a sleek black leather folder. "Check this out."

Lois opened the menu. Her eyes widened at the impressive list of entrees inside. The menu described each dish in clear, crisp print. Sharp color photos of fresh, appetizing food jumped out from every page.

"I had these professionally printed," said William. "I think they did a great job."

"They did, but it must have been expensive."

"Not really, and what I did pay was worth it." William took back the menu and they continued their tour.

To the right of the doors the same old booths ran along the big picture windows at the front of the restaurant. More booths ran along the wall across from the lunch counter. Though their original carpentry remained, it had been stained dark to match the new counter. Butcher block tables, also stained dark, now stood in place of the old worn and broken particle board and laminate ones. The same red leather that covered the bar stools also covered the booth benches.

The woodwork had been stained with care, but the dents and chips had not been sanded out. There were even dings and scratches in the new table tops.

The diner's old stained and torn carpeting had been pulled out. Now a four foot wide stripe of thick red plush carpet ran around the edges of the room, but a large square of parquet flooring covered the middle. Lois leaned down for a better look. Up close chips and scars were visible even through the floor's bright polish. In a few places it looked as though parts of the starburst pattern had been replaced with new wood that while close didn't quite match the original.

"Where did you get it?" Lois asked.

"We salvaged it from the ballroom of an old hotel in Detroit. Got the piano there, too."

William tilted his head towards the big round dais in the center of the floor. On it stood an antique Steinway Music Room Grand piano. It had been painted white, but the paint had been sanded down in places to let the instrument's original finish show through. Two florescent lights ran along the edge of it's open lid. Small ferns, ivy, and smooth polished river rocks filled the piano case. Some of the ivy's tendrils spilled over the edge. They reached nearly to the floor.

"Wow," Lois said.

"Just wait," said William. He pulled a remote control from his pocked and pressed a button. Soft piano music filled the air. He pressed a second button. Tiny multicolored fairy lights began winking on and off among the greenery. At the press of a third button jets of water shot up from between the rocks. They fell back into the piano

8

case in graceful arcs.

"How in the world..."

William smiled. "My best friend's an engineer, remember?"

Four staggered rings of small, black, round tables surrounded the dais. Two open back dining chairs flanked each table. The chair seats were upholstered in the same red leather as the booths and the counter stools. The color theme continued on with red cloth napkins, red place-mats, and a blood red rose in a crystal vase at the center of each table. Like the booth benches and tables, there were chips and dents in the lacquer finish of these tables and chairs. William saw Lois frown when she noticed it.

"Don't worry. It's on purpose," he told her.

"But why?"

William shrugged. "Just to show that stuff that's a little beat up can still be beautiful. Besides for the dinner service we use white tablecloths instead of the place-mats and add candles. No one notices the scars."

He led her around the dais to the back of the diner where a long bar ran across the wall separating the restaurant's dining area from the kitchen. Designed to match the lunch counter, it too was made from dark wood and had a white granite top. The same type of red stools sat in front of it. At the back of the bar intricately carved wooden arches framed large gilt trimmed mirrors. Thin wooden shelves crowded with liquor bottles ran across them. Overhead a sleek metal rack held stemware of varying shapes and sizes. Like everywhere else, there were obvious gouges in the front of the bar.

"Let me guess," said Lois. "You had the bar shipped over from some ancient pub in Dublin."

"Actually, I built it myself and just distressed it to make it look old. Got the mirrors from a place in Boston, though. And I actually found a bar tender in this hick town who knows how to make more than gin and tonics."

"Your friend Riley?"

"Yep. He's my assistant manager, too. I couldn't run this place without him."

In the back corner between the bar and the lunch counter a vintage phone booth straight out of the 1940s stood against the wall.

"Is that real?" Lois asked.

"Sure is. I replaced the glass and Riley rewired the phone. It makes calls and everything."

Lois gave him a puzzled look. "What's with this new passion for fixing up old stuff?"

"It's comforting, is all. I like proving that even something that got totally wrecked can be rebuilt and made new again."

"Like your life?"

"That's still a work in progress."

"You've come a long way so far."

"Yeah, but not far enough."

William looked out the window at the gas station across the street. Many years before, his girlfriend Annie Lewis had been shot and killed there and the place still brought back painful memories. He'd wanted to buy it and tear it down, but he couldn't do that and still buy the diner. Instead, William had paid the gas station's owner to install a cement bench in the spot where she had fallen. It had been expensive because it had meant relocating some of the gas pumps, but William considered every penny worth it. Annie's full name, date of birth and date of death were carved into the bench's back. There was also a copper plaque explaining the circumstances of her murder at the hands of the Casners' son Timmy. William never went over there, but he had a binding contract with the gas station owner insuring that the bench could never be removed.

"You can't live in the past, William."

"I'm not. Some things need to be remembered, but I am moving on. Actually, I'm dating Andrea again."

"Really? That's great! You two gonna have kids?"

"Shit, I haven't even thought about it. We don't have room for them right now. Her sister and two small nephews live at her place. That's why I live here instead of living with Andrea."

"You're living in the hotel rooms?"

"Not exactly. I converted them into a separate building to live in. It's just better to have to actually leave the diner to go home. It keeps the cooking smells out of the house."

"I bet. Doesn't it bother you to live where you work?"

"Not really. I did it when I worked here before. And it saves a ton of money. You could have done the same thing. Why didn't you?"

"Are you kidding? After twenty-five years you couldn't pay me to live here! And trust me, once you start turning a profit you won't want to either."

"Actually we're already turning a profit, but I want to put most of it back into the diner. We've fixed up the kitchen some, but it still needs work."

"Do I get to see the kitchen?"

"Right this way."

William led her through the swinging double doors next to the bar.

Most of the same old equipment still filled the kitchen, but it had been rearranged to make the work flow more smoothly. Broken items had been repaired and missing knobs and switches had been replaced. A new coating covered the concrete floor. Most impressively, everything was sparkling clean, including the walls and tight corners of the grill. The whole kitchen now smelled of fresh herbs and rich sauces instead of rancid grease.

"Not bad," said Lois.

"Thanks," said William. "Took us about a week but we finally got everything cleaned up back here."

"I admit I kind of let it go the last few years. Things just weren't the same after you left. I guess I just got tired. "

"Sooner or later I probably will, too, but for now I have to do everything I can to make this place work."

"Make sure you take full advantage of the tax laws like I taught you, then. Otherwise they'll rob you blind."

"Oh, I do. I donate to the community center and the high school and this crime prevention program called New Laws."

"What's that?"

"Well, it's basically an intervention program meant to reach kids who might get into trouble. These three guys go from school to school warning the kids about the dangers of drugs and gangs and give them alternatives to crime. From what I've heard they have really good success rates."

"Sounds like a great program. If they existed fifteen years ago maybe they would have helped you."

11

"Yeah, or maybe not having Lord Casner fighting with me."

"Yeah, that would have helped a lot, actually."

"You know this town changed so much since dictator Randy and Carol Casner fell from power. It was rough, anyone who didn't heil them got sent away to 'Ran-schwitz'. I got sent there lots of times and was forced to make hinges eighteen hours a day."

"Oh really?" Lois replied, getting the reference to Auschwitz. She remembered that William would often rant about his personal war with the Casners and give real war history references to it.

"Yep, and if I didn't make the hinges fast enough, the guards let me know about it. One time they timed me and I made one in good time. Then the guard said to me, 'let me get this straight, you can make a hinge in less than five minutes, and you been working here all day. Yet, such small pile of hinges! Take him out back and beat the shit outta him.' Oh man and did they ever!"

"Oh, wow, sounds terrible," Lois replied humoring yet another one of William's eccentric and bizarre war stories.

"But that was before they were defeated. After their fall of power the guards of 'Ran-schwitz' left. All the prisoners woke up and the gates were open and they were free."

"Wow, they should've had a parade for you." Lois enjoyed playing along with Williams fantasies. They laughed for a moment before growing quiet.

"Come out back. There's one more thing I want to show you."

Lois followed William out the back door. Behind the diner some odd, large object wrapped in a tarp lay on a flat bed trailer. William pulled the tarp loose. Underneath was a 6 ft wide diamond shaped sign mounted on a long metal pole. The light bulbs covering it spelled out "Moe's Diner" in elegant script.

"Where did you find that?"

"A junkyard in Nevada. Riley and I are trying to get it fixed. It'll rotate after it's installed."

"That is really cool," said Lois. "You are doing so well with this place. I really feel like I'm leaving it in good hands."

William looked at her sadly. "So you're really leaving town, huh?"

"Yes, took the money and paid off the house, stashed some in the bank and got enough for my Caribbean cruise."

"Well someday I'll do the same." William replied with a smile.

"Yeah, when you're older."

"I am older! It's amazing how things change. Do you know not even one teacher or administrator that was at the high school when I was there is still there? Not even one cop in town that I remember still works here. It's like a whole new town in the last fifteen years.

"Wait 'til you're my age you wanna see things change. When I opened this diner you could still smoke indoors and nobody had a cell phone," Lois replied.

"Yeah, I know. This town still sucks, but at least I can enjoy not being public enemy number one anymore. Heck, nobody even recognizes me anymore."

"Maybe you should try to keep it that way," Lois replied with the motherly smile William needed. They headed back inside. Both were convinced William would give the place the revival it needed. With a fashionable new look and twenty-five years of longevity Moe's diner could be a money making machine.

Chapter 2

Cheaters May Prosper

William stood at the diner's front window waving goodbye to Lois as she drove away. Watching her leave made him sad. He knew she'd return from her cruise eventually, but he felt like he might never see her again. Even though she'd fired him more times than either of them could count, Lois had always been one of the first to support him when he'd had a problem. A jolt of panic stabbed him when he realized that from now on she wouldn't be there to fix it if something went wrong. He was on his own.

Behind him, the diner's phone began to ring. He let it keep ringing as he watched Lois's car disappear down the highway. When she was finally out of sight he turned and picked up the receiver.

"Moe's Diner, this is William."

"Hey, William, this is Mr. Perez, the gym teacher at the high school."

"Oh, what's up?"

"Well, two things. First, I wanted to thank you again for the donation from the diner to the track team. Also, I just thought you should know this kid named Roger Delahoy may have broken your track record."

"He what? No way! What do ya mean 'may have'? He either broke it or he didn't. I've held that record for fourteen years."

"Oh boy! Roger was making up the mile run after school yesterday because he missed it in gym class last week. I was timing him, but then there was this loud boom that sounded like a gunshot so I went to check it out. Turns out it was nothing, just a car backfiring, but you know I had to check. Anyway, Roger kept running. He was just finishing a lap when I got back. He said it was his fourth and he was finished. That's when I checked the stopwatch and saw he had a time of 4:41. Your old time was 4:50, so it looks like we might have a new record."

"But there were no witnesses or anything?" asked William.

"No witnesses. That's why we haven't made it official yet. I'm supposed to meet with the school administrators in about half an hour. We'll decide then if the record will stand."

"Well they wanna give it to him huh? I'm on my way," William barked.

Although William still owned and loved his old 65 Lincoln with suicide doors, an older William now had a second car for more practical needs. His red Chevrolet Impala got it's rpm's almost to redline as he drove like a harebrained lunatic to the school.

"Where is he?" William demanded as he barged into the gym.

Mr. Perez met William at the door and held up a restraining hand. Being short and wiry, the gym teacher had to take a step back and tilt his head up to look William in the face. Despite the warm day, Mr. Perez wore a grey sweatshirt with the school logo on it and red sweat pants. Thick glasses that seemed too large for his face magnified his soft brown eyes. A thin fringe of salt and pepper hair surrounded his bald head. Smiling with teeth a little too white and too straight to be quite natural, he tried to calm William down.

"He's over there." Mr. Perez pointed to the far corner of the gym. "Please, William, let's just take a minute or two and sort everything out, okay?"

William defiantly stared at Roger. Everything from the kid's short legs, greasy black hair, dumpy, skinny body to his wannabe gang-banger clothes and cheap shoes gave William reason to suspect Roger had swindled the track record.

"No way," said William. "There's just no way that kid ran that fast."

"Well stranger things have happened," said Mr. Perez, but he sounded unconvinced. "The principal and vice principal are on their way over now. The three of us are going to take a vote on whether or not to let the record stand."

"How are you going to vote?"

Mr. Perez hesitated. "I can't say."

"Oh come on! You know there's no way he ran all four laps. You were distracted and there are no witnesses. You can't let him have that record."

"It's not that simple, William. I can't say he did it, but I can't say for sure that he didn't, either. If he really did it I hate to take it away from him."

"You're kidding me, right?"

"Let's just see what the others have to say, okay?"

Mr. Polk, the principal, and Ms Sanders, the vice-principal entered the gym. The two were as opposite as night and day. Principal Polk stood almost six feet tall with a short well groomed haircut and an elegant black power suit with a red tie. His conservative demeanor was illustrated in his clean shaven face, slight scowl on his mouth and rings on his finger of a cross and another with the Masonic G. William tried not to laugh at his big bubbly red nose. Polk ran his hand through his slicked back gray hair to gather his thoughts.

Mrs. Sanders, the vice principal showed she was close to William's age with her purple ladies' business suit and medium length blond hair. William assumed she was a bleeding heart liberal with her bright colors, the fact she would work at a high school, wore no make-up and the masculine look of her face and body.

Mr. Perez ushered everyone into his glass walled office at the side of the gym and shut the door.

Mr. Polk looked quizzically at William. "Who's this?"

"This is William Defreno, the former record holder," said Mr. Perez.

"Current record holder," William corrected.

Mr. Polk frowned. "What grade are you in, son?"

"I'm not a student here," said William. "I've held that record for 14 years. I own Moe's Diner."

"Oh, well you have to understand, when you get to be my age everyone looks like a teenager.'

"Ri-ight," William said skeptically.

Mrs. Sanders stepped forward and shook William's hand.

"Mr. Defreno, William, I just wanted to say what an honor it is to finally meet you. I really admire the way you stood up to the Casners.

That was very brave of you, especially for someone so young."

"Uh... Thanks," said William.

"Wait a minute!" shouted Mr. Polk. "You're that William Defreno?"

"As far as I know I'm the only William Defreno."

"Harris told me all about you! You've got some nerve barging into a school that expelled you, son!"

"That may be true, Mr. Polk, but I figured if my money was welcome then so was I."

Mr. Polk again turned to Mr. Perez. "What's he talking about?"

"Um, Mr. Defreno has been a very generous supporter of the track team this year, as well as the drama club and the culinary arts program."

"Don't forget New Laws," William interjected. "They've been a lot of help here, right?"

"They have indeed." Mrs. Sanders smiled. "Of course you're welcome here, William. We always appreciate community involvement in the school. Your being here is very helpful. And before he retired Harris did tell me he regretting expelling you."

Mr. Polk looked doubtful.

"And we in the athletic department are truly grateful for your continued support," Mr. Perez said with a tight smile on his face.

"Well, hmm." Mr. Polk began drumming his fingers on his sleeve. "We had pretty much decided to give Roger the record, but I see it's going to be a little more complicated."

"William," said Mrs. Sanders. "You've held that record for fourteen years. Don't you think it's time someone else got the chance?"

"Yeah, if they beat it fairly, but I don't think he did."

"You don't know for sure, William." Ms. Sanders looked through the glass at Roger standing alone in the corner of the gym. "Roger's a troubled boy. He's had some issues here. Having an accomplishment to be proud of might just be the thing that turns him around. I think he needs that record more than you do."

"You don't understand," said William. "Maybe to you it means nothing, to me it means everything. I got my leg broken because of that record. I got expelled from this school because of that record. I nearly went to prison because of that record. The girl I loved was murdered in front of me, all because of that record. Breaking it ended up costing me everything I had and now it's the only thing I have left to hold on to. I can't give it away just because some kid's a hard luck case."

"It's that important?"

"Yeah, it is." William looked from Mr. Perez, to Polk, and then back to Ms. Sanders. "Look if he broke my record once, he can do it again. All I'm asking for is a re-test, with witnesses. I think that's more than fair. If he even gets close to the time he got yesterday he can have it, but we're not doing this kid any favors by giving him the record if he didn't earn it."

They stared back at him in silence. Ms. Sanders looked unhappy. Mr. Perez looked anxious. Mr. Polk just looked bored. William decided it was time to pull out his ace in the hole.

"Uh, Mr. Polk," William said as he pulled a form out of his pocket. "I heard you were hoping to send the debate team to a competition in New York this summer, but were still a little short of the funds?"

"Ye-es," Mr. Polk said, suspiciously.

"Well it just so happens that I have some money left in my donation account and I have to use it if I want to get my IRS rebate this quarter."

"Really?"

"Yeah. The only catch is the quarter ends tomorrow so I have to make a donation today. So, I brought the form with me. If we can get this settled quickly I'll have time to fill it out and still get it to my accountant today. But if not, well the accountant will just have to pick someplace else to donate that money on his own."

"Oh." said Mr. Polk. Standing next to him, Mr. Perez looked slightly queasy.

"And of course I've left a little in reserve for the track team."

Mr. Perez smiled.

"Um, after considering all the facts, I have to agree that a re-test is only fair," said Mr. Polk.

"Really?" said Ms. Sanders. "We're going to let a fat check for the debate team decide a student's future?" She looked disgusted.

"Now, now," said Polk. "A lot of students' futures ride on that debate competition, too. It's nationally publicized, you know. A lot of our kids, and the school, will get noticed if our team does well."

"Unbelievable," said Ms. Sanders. She headed for the door. Just before leaving she turned to William. "And you should be ashamed of yourself! Bribery is beneath you."

Ms. Sanders slammed the office door on her way out. William suddenly felt badly. It seemed like Ms. Sanders had genuinely liked him and he'd just blown that, but he didn't know how else he was supposed to get through to Polk. He cleared his throat before addressing the two men still in the room.

"So we're agreed? Roger will retest tomorrow?"

"Absolutely," said Polk.

"I can have him run the trial at lunch tomorrow," said Mr. Perez. "And we'll make sure it happens right this time."

"Glad to hear it," said William. "Let me write you those checks."

On their way out they stopped to break the news to Roger.

"This is bullshit!" the kid screamed.

"Take it easy, son," said Polk.

"I ain't your son! Don't call me that! How come I gotta do it again? Just cause some guy with money don't like me taking his record?"

"Roger, we're asking you to do it again because it wasn't properly witnessed the first time," said Mr. Perez. "And Mr. Defreno has generously agreed to give you the record even if you don't beat his time again, so long as you come in within 20 seconds of your original time."

"Whatever. This blows, man!"

Roger stormed out of the gym. "Just you wait, man! Just you wait!" he yelled back at William.

"Was that a threat?" asked Polk.

"I think he was referring to the record," said Mr. Perez.

"I hope so," said Polk. "I wouldn't like to think a student here was coming unraveled and might do something violent. We worked hard to put those days behind us."

Mr. Perez kicked Mr. Polk lightly in the shin.

"What?" said Polk.

William just shook his head and walked out to his car.

As he drove away a feeling of relief washed over him. His record was still his. That track record was the only glory he had in high school that didn't involve infamy. He even remembered that he broke that track record before the war with the Casners started. That made it even more special to his memories of being that carefree kid with the world at his feet.

Ms. Sanders' words still stung, but there was anger along with the shame. If anything, William felt he was the victim, not Roger. All he did was stand up for himself. Bribing Polk may have been a low move, but William felt he shouldn't have had to stoop to that in order to be heard in the first place. It wasn't his fault that money was the only language Polk could understand.

William headed towards the diner, but the closer he got the less he felt like working that night. Instead, he called Riley to ask him to cover the dinner shift and then headed for Andrea's house.

Andrea's house was located in the same historic district where the small house he used to rent was. He drove past it every time he went to Andrea's. Although her house was medium size and boxy it's historic beauty and durability was easy to notice. The solid wood interior doors and rock hard plaster walls were still as strong as the day they were new over one hundred years ago. The place had a slight rust smell in the air from the original boiler still being used to heat the house. The bathrooms had been added on later because it had only had an outhouse when it was first built.

Andrea had bought her first house on the outskirts of town. When financial trouble hit her she was forced to sell it and move to a smaller one downtown. At one time the house's close to downtown location was considered unattractive. Due to recent urban renewal efforts by the city it was now considered convenient and close to everything. She recently found out that although the house was a downgrade in price from her other home, it was now worth more than her bigger, newer other house had been because of the location.

As he entered the house sounds of adults and kids indicated that everyone was home.

"Hello you guys," William said as he entered the house. He handed Andrea a bag with two soda bottles he'd picked up on the way and leaned over to kiss her hello.

Andrea and Shelly were in the dining room while the little boys ran around the house screaming. Often people would get Andrea and her sister Shelly mixed up since they looked so identical with the same sparkling green eyes, smooth, silky face and long brown hair parted in the middle. Both had good wholesome hourglass figures and noticeable curves in the right places.

If it were not for the fact that Andrea was older and a little taller they would be close to identical twins. William always said Shelly was just Andrea shrunk to 80%.

Their brother Geoff was in the other room ranting about his favorite team the Dodgers losing to the Mets. He could overhear Geoff say, "What, they all need another hundred grand a game before they can hit the damn ball?" William just smiled to himself until he heard a familiar voice.

"Oh geez, you drive a loser Impala?"

William looked to see it was the horrible Melissa girl that aggravated him through high school. If it were not for Andrea liking her she would be a distant putrid memory in his mind. Her dumpy body, a face dried out from too much Marijuana use took away any chance of her ever being attractive. Hearing her nasty voice again was like nails on blackboard.

"Loser Impala? What do you drive?"

"I don't drive, but any guy who gets to date me would have to pick me up in a Bentley, a stretch Bentley," Melissa replied in her same delusional tone that matched her over-inflated ego.

"I'll give you a bent lip, I mean a Bentley," William joked holding up his fist.

"Oh stop, William," Andrea said.

William just shook his head at the fact that Andrea didn't stand up for him, but instead defended Melissa. His mind was dominated by Roger possibly beating his track record and didn't have room to fight with Melissa over stupid things. William, Andrea, Shelly, Geoff, Melissa and the two boys, Thomas and his slightly older brother Phillip sat down to eat. Geoff sat at the end of the table.

William was glad her brother Geoff had come over for dinner. Being 6 feet tall with a nice two hundred and thirty pound build, brother Geoff could eat more than his two sisters put together. Geoff, with his clean shaven, over tanned face and long blond hair down to his shoulders, glared at the little boys with his brown eyes because they would not calm down.

William wondered why at ages seven and nine the little boys could not comprehend that Uncle Geoff was getting very angry at their undomesticated behavior. Both of them being cute and adorable was not an excuse for them to keep pinching each other and saying unintelligible words that they thought were funny. They both looked very identical and were referred to as "the boys" rather than by their individual names. When dinner was served Thomas threw some dirt from a nearby plant at Phillip.

"Ahhh!!" Phillip screeched and threw the dirt back at Thomas.

"Ewww, yuck," Thomas screamed back as the two of them started hitting each other. The table shook as they struggled with each other and knocked over Geoff's glass of soda. He quickly stopped the soda from spilling on the new limited edition L.A. Dodgers jersey he was wearing. A deep breath was taken that not one drop of soda had hit the jersey. The two of them didn't even notice they had spilled the drink.

"Yo!" Geoff bellowed "Calm the fuck down!"

"Geoff, please," Shelly said pleadingly.

"What do you feed these little pieces of shit for breakfast? A kilo of cocaine?"

"They're just children, ya know," Shelly responded.

Even though Geoff had yelled loud enough to cause everyone's ears to ring it had minimal effect on the little boys. Both of them just ignored the fact that they almost ruined his clothes and were disturbing dinner. Geoff was the oldest child in the family with a seven year age gap between him and middle child Andrea and ten years between him and Shelly.

"Hey," Geoff said. "Have you forgotten that when we were all kids they we had to sit up straight and shut up at the dinner table? If we wanted something we would have to say something like 'please pass the carrots' and 'thank you, Sir or Ma'am.' When dinner was over we had to say 'may I please be excused.' What would our parents have done if we caused a disturbance like that?"

"Just calm down, Geoff," Andrea said.

Finally things settled down around the dinner table. Andrea and Shelly had cooked a meal made to please, serving up plates of lasagna with salad, steamed carrots and fresh garlic bread. Though the girls had been cooking for hours, Melissa had done nothing to help and brought no food or beverages. William wondered if that upset Andrea as much as it did him. With everyone seated and food on their plates conversation began.

"Lois was amazed at the way I cleaned up Moe's diner," William said to everyone.

"I know," Geoff added. "The place doesn't smell like ass anymore."

"What did you pay for the place?" Melissa asked.

"I can't disclose that," William said. He knew no matter what he said she would say he got ripped off and that she could've gotten it cheaper.

"That place sucks, your customers are all losers," Melissa continued.

"It's looking pretty nice these days," Andrea answered.

"You don't have any business skills, you shouldn't have bought it," Melissa said.

"Whatever," William replied and wondered if Geoff had the same thought he had; what is this moron doing at our dinner table?

"What did you learn in school today?" Shelly asked her boys.

Phillip opened his mouth full of food and said "Blaaa."

For some reason Shelly smiled at their buffoonery. After William saw that even Andrea didn't mind the appalling table manners he decided to just tell everyone what he'd been doing all day.

"I learned in school today that someone can break a fourteen year old track record without it being verified," William said.

"What do you mean?" Andrea said.

"If I hadn't gone down to the school today they would've given away my track record. The gym teacher was timing him, got distracted by what he thought was gunshots and lost count of how many laps this kid did. The kid said he did all four but I call bullshit on that."

"Are you just saying that 'cause you don't want your record taken away?" Shelly asked.

"I'm really not. I was told that it was broken many years ago. Turned out it wasn't, but I wasn't upset when I thought it had been. If he is better than me fine, but the kid had like ten dollar sneakers on. If you ran that hard on those cheap shoes they would fall apart. He had chicken legs and looked really devitalized. He wasn't healthy enough to run like that. Not just that, he just looked like a little shyster. I mean the world record for the mile is like 3:30 and mine was only a little over a minute more than that. Not to brag, but it's gonna take a hell of an athlete to beat that record."

"Could they retest him?" Andrea asked.

"Thanks to me they're going to. They were just gonna take his word that he did it. I bet tomorrow he doesn't get anywhere close to my record."

"Only dorks run track," Melissa blurted out.

"That can't be true," William replied. "I've never seen you run it."

"You're such an ass, William," Melissa replied. "If I were Andrea I'd dump yer ass."

"And be single like you?" William replied.

"I'm not going to be single for long, Brad Pitt is gonna marry me."

"Does Angelina know?" Geoff asked.

"I wrote to him and he send me an autographed picture of himself and it said that he thought I was cute."

Geoff laughed, "That's called an auto reply. His secretary sent that."

"Anyway," William continued. "The vice principal made me feel like I was being a jerk or petty or something. I know it's a high school track record but it means a lot to me and I trained hard to get it. It shouldn't just be something they give away like it's nothing."

"You did the right thing," Andrea said. "If he could do it once he can do it again."

William felt satisfied that he was doing the right thing by standing up for his record. After dinner was done the main dishes were cleared and it was time for strawberry shortcake for dessert. Melissa didn't help clear the table, but instead barked orders at everyone to help.

After the cake was cut all the slices were put on plates. Little Thomas grabbed one only to have older brother Phillip take it.

"That's mine!" Thomas whined

"Not anymore," Phillip said with a giggle.

"Phillip, give that back to Thomas! Here's one for you," Shelly said to them. Both pieces of cake were the same size with the same amount of strawberries on them, but they still fought. William realized it had nothing to do with one being better than the other, they just wanted an excuse to fight.

"I don't want that one, I want this one," Phillip cried out.

"But it's mine!" Thomas whined and began to cry "Gimme it!"

"No, you can have that one!"

"Waaa, I don't want that one, butthead!"

The two of them fighting over the cake caused the plate to tip and the red strawberry juice to splatter on Geoff's Dodgers jersey. William knew that wearing a nice clean expensive jersey to dinner would be regretted around there. Geoff looked down and then looked at the boys with wide cat eyes. The look was bloodcurdling. William could imagine a mushroom cloud from an atomic bomb going off in Geoff's head. The boys were oblivious to it and kept fighting.

"Jesus H. Goddamn Christ!" Geoff roared as he snatched both plates away from them. "Now none of you get cake, you little sons of bitches!"

Both of them ran to the kitchen where Shelly and Andrea were cleaning up the dinner mess. The lasagna pan would need some hard scrubbing to get the remnants off. Both girls had to be careful not to put too much stuff down the hundred year old drains. The boys did a magnificent job of looking like they've been terribly victimized by someone as they came into the kitchen. Phillip was so upset he couldn't even say anything. His words sounded like grunts. Shelly stopped what she was doing to see what could make them so upset.

"Uncle," Sniffle, sniffle. "Uncle Geoff stole our caaaake," Thomas whined as he started bawling. Before she could reply Geoff came in and showed the stains on his shirt.

"Geoff, take it off and we'll put some stain remover on it and wash it," Shelly said.

"You gonna be okay, Geoff?" William asked as Geoff walked by him to the laundry room. His eyes were wide open and glazed over with rage.

"I'm just visualizing myself beating those kids with meat hooks."

William kept some clothes at Andrea's house and since he and Geoff were close to the same build his shirt would fit him while the Dodgers Jersey was in the wash. As Geoff came back to the dining room his face turned red when he saw the two boys eating the exact plates of cake he'd taken away from them. Shelly, Andrea, William and Melissa were at the dining table enjoying their desserts as well. When Geoff's shirt was done being washed he put on even though it was wet.

"I'm going home. Thanks for dinner," Geoff said to the group.

"Bye, see you," Andrea, Shelly and William replied.

"Oh and tell the boys if a stranger offers them candy or a ride to go ahead and take it."

"Geoff," Shelly replied in an irritated tone as he went to the door snickering to himself. The boys were done with their forbidden dessert and getting ready for bed. They could hear the loud engine of Geoff diesel truck. With Geoff gone and the boys in bed the four of them enjoyed coffee and William and Andrea got to smoke.

"Ralphie is coming back to town pretty soon," Melissa said.

"Oh yeah, I remember him," Andrea said.

"Yeah, he dropped out of school when he was sixteen," William added.

"Well he's got some huge job he's getting here and he called and wants a place to stay for a few weeks," Melissa said.

"Why not stay with you?" William said to Melissa.

"Yeah, right, like my stupid parents are gonna let him live with us. Besides our love is dead. Me and Ralph one were once on top of the world, living a fairy tale. It was Romeo and Juliet, but then our world crashed down. But I'll never forget our intense memories of our prime," Melissa stated.

"Didn't you guys only date for a week?" Andrea asked.

"Yeah, six days. Then the bastard drove me out to the middle of nowhere and left me stranded. He's so hot tempered, kinda like William and your brother. I was just telling him the truth, trying to be open and honest with him. You can't be open and honest with men without 'em being assholes"

"Open and honest about what?" William asked.

"That his stupid motorcycle is a piece of shit. It's not my fault it's a piece of shit. He had a stupid haircut too."

"Oh my God," William said as he put his hand over his face. "Did Ralph ask your opinion of his motorcycle or haircut?"

"No, but I couldn't help it. His bike was a loser-mobile. I was just trying to do the dickhead a favor and tell him the truth. Men suck. Cats are so much better."

"Ya know," William protested. "Did you ever think that maybe not everyone needs to hear you insult everything about them? You don't even have a car, or a job or a place to live besides yer parents house. You don't have the right to talk shit to everyone else. Yer in yer thirties now, maybe it's time to stop acting like some spoiled brat teenager."

"William, stop," Andrea said. "Anyway Melissa, if Ralph can pay some rent I could give him room and board here."

"Yeah he should be able to pay rent. I don't know how much, though. This job he's getting sounds like loser job. He said it only pays like two hundred grand a year. That's why I wouldn't take him back. Like I'm gonna date some low income loser."

William rolled his eyes again. Same old Melissa from high school. As much as things changed in the city at least some things stayed the same. The only good thing about Melissa being there was it gave him something to be mad about so he wouldn't obsess on Roger and the track record. He was confident Roger would never be able to beat it tomorrow and would feel foolish demanding a retest if he did beat it again.

After coffee and cigarettes it was time to let Andrea and Shelly go to bed.

"Oh, William, will you take Melissa home on you're way back to the diner?" Andrea asked.

"I guess."

William warmed up the car and decided not to say even one word to Melissa to avoid pointless fighting, though he knew it would probably be inevitable. Odds were she would somehow make sure that he would live to regret taking her home.

27

The radio was turned up loud and it looked like he would make it back to her house without incident. She was playing with her phone and looking at his radio.

"Why do you go out with Andrea?"

"Cause I like her."

"Why? She's ugly and her house smells like a rusty piece of shit."

"Whatever."

"Her sister's ugly too. Why don't you get a real girlfriend?"

William didn't even answer and turned up the radio to block the unnecessary noise coming from Melissa. William laughed that Michael Jackson's "Beat It" was playing. He thought Andrea should tell Melissa to "never ever come around here" and wished she would "beat it." She was fiddling with her phone and looking at his radio. Whatever she was doing it was probably trouble. William sped up to try to get her home as fast as he could.

"William, your stupid thermometer is wrong."

"What do you mean?"

"My phone says that the temperature in this city is seventy five degrees, you're car says it seventy-three."

"Well, you're phone is picking up the temp of the city. That thermometer could be miles from here. The car is picking up the temperature right outside the car."

"Why would it vary two degrees in the same city?"

"Well, it can vary all over. Literally, I've seen it change up to six or seven degrees just from the diner to Andrea's house. It does that. The whole city isn't exactly the same temperature. Look on your phone and see where it's picking up the reading from."

"You're so fuckin' stupid, William. Your goddamn thermometer's not right. Quit trying to make excuses. It's a piece of shit just like this car. How much did you pay for this car, anyway?"

"None of your business."

"Well you got ripped off. You should go down to the dealership and tell them to fix this thermometer."

"Oh yeah, right. This car is six years old. They're not gonna re-calibrate the thermometer to match your phone."

"They would for me. I'd tell 'em I'm gonna sue them if they don't and that they better fuckin' do it. But I guess yer a big fuckin' wimp, so they wouldn't do it for you."

William could feel the same atomic mushroom cloud in his head that Geoff had earlier in the evening. The wise thing to do would be to just drop her off at her house that was less than a mile away. An internal struggle went on in his head of whether to just get her home or tell her off without Andrea taking her side. He decided for now to let it go.

"What are you going to do about the thermometer?" Melissa demanded.

"You really can't see the fact that you're phone that is going off of a thermometer miles from here is going to read differently that the car that's picking it up right here?" he yelled.

"You're so fucking stupid!" She screamed. "You wont admit your car sucks and you got ripped off. Go down to the fuckin' dealership and tell them to fix the fuckin' thermometer. Or are you to much of a pussy?"

"Who the fuck cares? Even if the damn thing was inaccurate what difference does it make? Why are you screeching in my ear about it? It doesn't matter!"

"I'm just trying to help you. Losers like you need all the help they can get."

"I don't need jack diddly from you!"

"All men need help. You're all defective and stupid. I can't believe you would buy a car without making sure the thermometer was accurate. Yer such a loser."

"Here," William screamed as he covered the temperature reading on the radio with his hand. "Don't even look at it. It's covered up."

In a brief silence William wondered why the music stopped playing. Unaware of his own strength and being completely enraged, he didn't know that when he put his hand over the temperature display he had hit the radio unit with his hand. The unintentional impact was so hard it had broken the crystal display and shorted the whole radio unit out. All that was displayed now was cracked gibberish.

"Oh good job, dumbass, you broke it," Melissa said in a snotty tone.

William was about a microsecond away from bashing her skull in with his fist. He was certain that her behavior was planned and premeditated and needed to be punished. He slammed on the brakes with both feet. The car's wheels locked up and the car weaved out of control before it came to a halt. Melissa went flying forward but unfortunately didn't hit her head on the dashboard. William put the car in park, opened his door and walked to the front of it.

"What now? God, you are such an idiot," Melissa continued.

"There's a good two hundred bucks down the drain for a new radio you stupid fuckin' dickweed!" William shouted at her standing at the front of his car while she stayed inside.

"It was broken anyway."

"Oh Eli Eli lama sabachthani," William continued yelling at her.

"What?"

"It's Hebrew for 'my God my God why have you forsaken me?' I mean how could God allow such a horrible atrocity like the thermometer being inaccurate to happen? Sabachthani, sabachthani, sabachthani," William yelled in a cynical tone.

"Oh, you're not one of those morons who believes in God are you?" Melissa continued.

"Not anymooooore," He yelled louder. "You just wont quit will you? Just shut up!"

"You need anger management. Really, William, you need to see a shrink. I'm just trying to show you something and you freak out. Besides, there is no God, dumbass."

"Oh, how the hell would you know? You don't even know that your stupid phone thermometer reading comes from somewhere else in the city. It doesn't magically know the exact temperature outside of the car while yer sitting inside the car. But you know for a fact there is no God."

"Well, I'm way smarter than you," Melissa said.

"Yer right, there can't be a God. If there was how could he allow such a thing as the thermometer in the car to be off by two mother fucking lousy degrees? It's not even off! Only an imbecile would think the phone is going to read out the same exact reading as the car."

By now people in the neighborhood were peeking out their windows and even coming outside. William looked around and saw that the interior and exterior lights in the whole row of houses were turning on in sequence. William knew that curiosity was building fast toward the man standing in front of his car screaming biblical quotes to the passenger inside.

It could be assumed the cops were probably on their way. Even though he wanted to scream more at her, it was not worth a visit to the jail for it. It was unclear to him if any of this screaming was doing any good. He got back in the car and peeled out and drove to her mom's house.

"Get out!" William said in a tone that unintentionally sounded like The Terminator.

William went back to the diner and to his house on the property. It was worth a little demolition to make the house part a separate building from the diner. Now he could technically say he didn't live in the diner. The six hundred square foot building had everything he needed including a bathroom, bedroom and small kitchenette. It was small but easy to clean and if he needed food or booze he could go and get it easily. Tonight he decided to go into the diner itself and sit at the bar for a few drinks. Those few drinks turned into a few too many drinks. He knew his drinking habit was starting to become more than just a once in a while thing. After a day like today he realized this would not be the night he would decide to quit.

The next afternoon the lunch shift was busy. Luckily Riley was bursting with energy to make up for Williams slacking. Riley kept a cool head about having to do both of their jobs on a busy day, but his sympathy was about to expire. Finally the cell phone rang. William hoped it would be the school calling but it was Andrea.

"Hello," William answered.

"So honey, I heard you almost got arrested last night."

"You mean because of your friend and I repeat *your* friend Mel."

"Yeah, she said you freaked out on her."

William instantly told her the whole story of breaking the radio and Melissa's conduct. He emphasized the point that not only would a new radio be about two hundred dollars but he would have to cut out of work early to go have it fixed. Riley was already being overworked as it was. It didn't seem like she would give him the response of "I'm gonna kill that bitch" or "she's gonna be sorry" that he wanted.

"She would not stop. She just kept it up and kept it up and kept it up," William protested.

"Well, she can be handful sometimes, but you don't need to freak out like that."

"A handful? She's an idiot, she always has been that way. She's not even that nice to you. She said I should get a real girlfriend."

"Well, anyway just cool it. Ralph is coming over today to see if he wants to rent out some room here till he gets his job thing going."

"Where is he gonna sleep, the carport? You already got a full house there."

"Well, that's up to him. We'll have to see. It probably won't even be for that long maybe a few weeks till he get a paycheck. With a two hundred grand a year job he should be able to get an apartment with one check."

"Yeah, what loser only makes two hundred grand a year? What a bum," William said, mocking Melissa's comment from the night before.

"Oh, quit picking on Mel. Anyway, he'll probably be here if you're coming over tonight. Oh, and let me know if that kid beats your record."

"Okay, see you tonight, sugar cookie."

Chapter 3

Against the Wind

William paced behind the bar, staring into space- lost in thought. He knew there was work he should be doing. They were short a busboy, the couple at table six needed their glasses refilled, and the old man at the bar was ready for his check. Still, he left Riley running around to cover for him while he stared at the walls. He got his orders in and delivered to their tables without really thinking about it. Neither the staff nor customers picked up on his distant state of mind. Riley could tell, though. William knew his best friend and manager could be trusted to cover for him while he was distracted. He suspected Riley's patience might be wearing thin, though.

Never in the history of the world had time moved so slowly. Finally at half past twelve the phone rang. Riley answered. He brought William the phone. William looked down at it as if it were a poisonous snake. He could feel butterflies in his stomach and a cold, clammy sweat breaking out of his forehead.

"Come on, William, it doesn't matter either way," said Riley.

"Yeah, yer right," said William, but his hand still shook as he took the receiver.

"This is William."

"Hey, William, Mr. Perez here."

"The jury's back huh? What's the verdict?"

"He retested at over six minutes, not even close to the other day."

"So that's it? My record stands?"

"Yeah, the semester ends for summer break next week so your record is safe for a while."

"I knew it! I wasn't trying to put the kid down, but I could just

33

tell by looking at him he didn't have it in him to do it."

"Yeah, it was obviously a mistake. He's not taking it well. He claims the wind was against him."

"What?"

"Well, it was windy today. He claims the headwind slowed him down."

"It's a round track! A headwind in one direction is a tailwind in the other. They'd even each other out."

"Yeah, well I don't think weather science is Roger's strong suit. He's not much of an academic. I told him he can try again in September, if he doesn't drop out by then."

Something nagged at the back of William's brain. "Yesterday Ms. Sanders said he was a troubled kid. What did she mean?"

"Oh, just the usual. He's truant a lot- been busted for pot a couple of times."

"And he expected us to believe he ran the mile that fast with bud in his lungs? Ya know, if he spent that weed money on decent running shoes and some nutrition drinks maybe he'd be able to beat me fairly."

"Well, that's the school counselor's problem, not mine. Thanks again for the donation to the track team. I will call you if anyone ever does break the record."

"Hopefully I'll be dead by then," William said with a nervous laugh.

"You never know, that's a pretty good time and I'm sad to say kids are less in shape now then they were fifteen years ago when you were in school."

"Well, thanks again. Talk to you next year."

William ended the call. A feeling of relief came upon him as he realized his glory days of running track in high school still mattered. With the worry about his record out of the way he bounced back quickly and started taking some of the work load off of Riley. The rest of the lunch shift passed in a blur. A last minute rush kept them open a bit later than usual, but finally the tables were cleared and the last of the dishes washed.

"Hey, Riley," said William. "I called the dealership about my radio. They actually have an opening now so if I get down there I can be back before we open for dinner. I may be a little late, though."

"No problem. Just make sure you keep your phone on in case the cook doesn't show up again."

"You got it."

William headed out to the parking lot. He stopped in his tracks when he saw the strange object on his car. He could have almost thought it was just trash left behind, except that it was sitting right in the middle of the hood. Looking closer, William saw that the odd shaped thing was actually two objects stacked on top of each other; a broken eight-track cartridge and an old 45 record. He picked them up and discovered that the record was glued to the eight-track. That wasn't his only surprise. He tried to put them down and soon realized they were now both stuck to his hand.

"Great!" he shouted. He headed back into the diner to find Riley.

"Hey, Riley, gimme a hand here." He held up the hand with the objects glued to it.

"What the hell?"

"I don't know, man. I picked it up and now it glued to my hand."

"Wow!" Riley said as he tried to pull the record out of William's hand.

"Oww," William replied.

"Alright, look." Riley checked his watch." We still have a little over an hour before the dinner seating. I'll drop you off at the urgent car, take the car to the dealership and then come pick you up, okay?"

"Yeah," William replied not even caring that this would likely mean they would be behind schedule for the dinner shift. It actually took a little maneuvering to get in the car with this object on his hand. It seemed weird to him to be a passenger in his own car. Once again he tried to get his hand free, but it only caused him pain. As they drove there was only one topic to talk about.

"What asswipe would do that?" Riley wondered.

"I don't know."

"Ya know, some stupid little kids think this is funny, but it's not. Now the diner could lose money and you have to go pay a doctor. How can kids just pick someone at random like this? It could've been anyone."

"I'm glad they didn't bust the windows or something. Weirdness, that's all I can say."

"Yeah, where would a kid even find an eight-track or a forty-five?"

"And why glue them together? What would you even call this thing, a broken eight-track record?" William said and made one last attempt to pull the thing off his hand. "Piss," William said as he realized his efforts were futile.

"Whoa, what did you say, William?"

"I said 'piss.'"

"No, before that."

"I don't know."

"You said a broken eight-track record. What's on the record and eight-track?"

"Um," He turned his hand palm up and read the song title on the record. "'The Long Run' by the Eagles." He had to flip his hand over, bend his elbow and point his fingers at himself to see the title on the eight-track. "And 'Against the Wind' by Bob Seger. Hey, I know that one! It goes 'runnin' against the wind, against the wind...'" The way William sang it made it clear he had no musical talent whatsoever.

"And 'The Long Run'? How does that go?"

"'Who can go the distance? We'll find out in the long run...'"

"Oh wow," said Riley. He looked at William with his eyes wide open and a look of astonishment on his face.

"What?" said William, "what am I missing?"

"'The Long Run'? 'Against the Wind'? Broken. Track. Record. It was Roger! Had to be!"

"Oh, that little pot-smokin', chicken legged-- Real clever! Wow, how creative" William said with as much sarcasm as he could.

"Yeah, the next generation are some real geniuses, huh?" Riley said with sarcasm as well.

They arrived at the doctor and Riley drove to the dealership. They both had some good luck as far as time goes; no wait for either of them. A little over an hour later they arrived back at the diner with a fixed radio and the ironic broken-track-record object removed from William's hand.

William and Riley kept their composure well as the rest of the staff came in. Even with them starting late the dinner shift began smoothly. With a sore red hand William just did his work and was happy that the radio and doctor visit were over. The thought of calling the city police just seemed to foreign to him due to his past encounters. Instead, he would probably swear a lot over it and make empty threats to Riley about what he's like to do to Roger.

"Alright I'm outta here, see you tomorrow," William said to Riley as the clock struck seven. He drove to Andrea's house almost excited to tell her about his day. All he could hope for was that his hard day would not get worse by having to see Melissa there screaming at him about things.

"What happened to your hand?" Andrea asked as he came through the door. After he was sure Melissa was not there he explained the whole story of the broken track record. He had to explain it twice because the odd details were just too hard to believe.

"That is so immature," Shelly said.

"Yeah I'm gonna get that little son of a bitch if it's the last thing I do," William said knowing it was an empty threat.

"Hey William, that really sucks," a man's voice said. William saw it was Ralph. Ralph and William were the same age, but Ralph looked older than a guy in his thirties with a goatee and long gray hair. Even though William had always been clean shaven, the two shared some of the same facial features. The only difference was Ralph had brown eyes and William had blue eyes. William was a little taller and had a thicker more muscular build.

William looked around the living room and saw Ralph had brought six garbage bags of stuff. One of the open bags revealed lots of VHS tapes and road maps. The other bags were just clothes. A closer look showed the clothes were mostly leather motorcycle gear and a pair of thick combat boots. On the sofa William saw Ralph's prized possession, an acoustic guitar in it's case.

When Geoff came over he glanced at everyone and then back at the stuff all over the floor. He didn't know what to ask about first, William's red hand or the guitar and garbage bags of items all over the place. He turned and looked at Andrea.

"Where'd ya get all the shit?" Geoff asked.

"It's Ralph's. He's gonna stay here till he gets his first paycheck."

Although William had always remembered Ralph being

rambunctious, at least Melissa wasn't invited to dinner tonight. The girls set all the food on the table and more than once almost fell over because the little boys would not get out of their way. With the main dish of meatloaf served everyone was once again ready for conversation. William noticed Geoff was in a decent mood.

"Don't forget I'm leaving for Cincinnati next week," Geoff said.

"I remember," Andrea replied. "I'll go over and feed your cat 'n stuff."

"How long will you be gone?" Shelly wondered.

"Prolly five or six days. Depends on the roads."

"You gonna drive?" William asked.

"Yeah, even though the damn tolls are higher than the gas."

"Hey at least now you don't have to pay a toll to get in and out of this city," William said.

"There used to be a toll to get in and out of town?" Shelly asked.

"Yep, and all the money would go to Randy and Carol Casner."

"Oh yeah," Geoff said in a sarcastic tone.

"Hey, if you own the town you can charge everyone who wants to come and go from it and buy more police officers with it," William continued.

"What's in Cincinnati?" Ralph wondered.

"Baseball convention. Six hall-of-famers are gonna be there and they think even Pete Rose will show."

"Whose that?" Shelly wondered.

"The guy I have a poster of in my kitchen."

"You're lucky that you can have a Pete Rose poster on your wall," William interrupted.

"What?" Geoff said.

"Well, it used to be that everyone in town could only have pictures and posters of Randy and Carol Casner on their walls and they had to have lots of different ones."

"Oh yeah?" Geoff replied with a smile.

"Yep, and if anyone ever asked which picture of them was your favorite, you were wise to always reply 'they're all my favorite.'"

"Anyway," Shelly said. "I've had enough city history lessons. What's so special about this Pete Rose guy?"

"He was in the hall of fame but got kicked out for gambling

money in Vegas against his team in 1989. Kicked him out of baseball and pulled him from the hall of fame a few years later. I don't think that was fair. I mean, he was a dirtbag for betting against his own team. He was gonna try to intentionally make his team lose to win money, but he still broke those records. He entered the hall of fame legally, unlike Barry Bonds."

"Barry Bonds?" Shelly said.

"Yeah, he broke the home run record, but tested positive for steroids. I think Roger Maris should get that record back. He may not have hit as many home runs but he did it without steroids."

"Yeah, these athletes and their damn steroids," Andrea added.

"Roger Maris is the man! I wonder what my card is worth? I've never had it appraised," Geoff continued.

Ralph stopped eating for a second and darted his eyes at Geoff and said "What card?"

"I have a 1958 Roger Maris rookie card in mint condition. It was rated at a ten, which is almost impossible."

"Why?" Ralph wondered.

"The highest rated card in the era is like a nine. To get a ten rating it has to be perfectly centered, have vibrant color, crisp cardboard, sharp corners and nice tint. It's not because of how it was taken care of, but they were just like Cracker Jack toys basically. They were made cheap, nobody knew they would be so valuable someday. The cards were not made centered and with good color and sharpness, they were made cheap and defective. That's why having one that just so happen to be made perfect and was kept perfect is a miracle."

"Wow, a ten rating," Ralph said, still devoting his entire attention to Geoff. "I would sure keep something like that safe, wouldn't just leave it lying around."

"It's safely tucked between the box spring and mattress. I'll probably have it appraised one day."

Ralph went back to his dinner and didn't ask anything more about baseball or Roger Maris. The subject was easily snuffed as the little boys started acting up again at the table. It was unclear what they were even fighting about this time. Shelly separated the two of them and they conducted themselves a little better.

"So what's this job of yours?" William asked Ralph.

"Oh, um, construction management for high rise commercial buildings."

"You have that kind of experience?" Andrea wondered.

"Oh, hell yeah! I was head project manager of the new World Trade Center."

"Really?" Shelly said with astonishment.

"Oh yeah. I had a big crew, but they were stupid and lazy. I pretty much build the damn thing myself."

"Wow, that's a big project. You did that by yourself?" Shelly said with even more excitement.

"How'd you get the antenna on top of it?" William asked with much skepticism in his voice.

"I strapped it to my back and carried it up there."

William let out a small laugh. After a few seconds he didn't know whether Ralph was just kidding around and being funny or if he was really that senseless. William wondered what everyone else thought of such an assertion. Nobody else seemed to have any reaction to it at all. He didn't know if that was good or bad. It wasn't the most important thing in the world, but not something to ignore, either.

"Wow," Shelly finally said. "You must have a strong back."

Once again William just couldn't decide if she was playing along, or actually thought Ralph's statements were true. While dinner was being cleaned up William laughed to himself. Earlier in the day at the diner he had heard the song he liked called "Sixth Ave Heartache" by The Wallflowers. One of the lyrics was, "I had my world strapped against my back." In his mind he had changed the lyrics for Ralph to, "I had my antenna strapped against my back."

William went back home when everything was done. Like before, the night ended with him sitting at the closed diner bar helping himself to some whiskey and cigarettes. Although the habits were bad for his health, this was his only time to relax all day. Finally, after a few too many he left and went back to his house. On the way he saw a young man in the alley. It only took a second to recognize him.

"Roger! What do ya think yer doin' here?" William demanded.

"Oh look who it is, the fastest man in the world!"

"You better use those legs and get outta here."

"I bet you couldn't catch me if you tried."

"I'm not gonna try. What are you doing here? Besides trespassing, that is."

"Man, why did you ruin my life?"

"What?" William said as he threw his hands up.

"I beat your record, man. I ran those four laps. It's not my fault the stupid gym teacher didn't keep track of it."

"You got to try again and you didn't even come close. I call bullshit."

"Man, you know how in football when the kicker has to make a long field goal and right before he kicks it the other team calls time out to mess with him? It usually works; the kicker can make it once but because he was duped by the other team and had to kick it again he misses the second time. That's what you did to me. I did terrible the second time. Plus, I was running against the wind."

"You little fuckin' smartass, I'm gonna run my foot against your ass!" William barked.

"I mean it, man! The wind was messin' with me the second try."

"Oh, come on! If you did it once you could've done it again. All you had to do was come close and we'd have believed you. Your time was that of someone who only ran three laps."

"I tried, but having to do it all over killed my moral and spirit. I can't even try again till September and who knows if I can do it again."

"Train and do it."

"You don't get it! It was a fluke. For some reason that day I just had it in me. I just did it, it just happened. Haven't you ever had a good day where everything went your way? That was me, but I couldn't have two good days."

"Even if that were true, you're not really a track star if it was some lucky fluke."

"So what? I did it that day. I don't have to be able to do it every day of my life. If a martial artist passes a black-belt test he probably can't pass one everyday, but if he does it once he keeps the black-belt forever. I did it once and you stole it away like some jealous prick."

"I still don't believe you did it. You only ran three laps."

"I did and you couldn't stand it. You have a diner, a girl, two cars. I got nothing, all I had was that record and you had to have that, too."

William began to have a sinking feeling that he may have stolen this kid's glory away from him. Yet, it was still a fact that if he didn't actually break the record he didn't deserve it no matter how bad he wanted it. All he wanted was for this kid to admit he cheated so he wouldn't have to feel like a bully taking his one thing in life away from him.

"Look, Roger, it's over now. Just admit you lied and I'll wish you all the luck in the world come September."

"Not gonna happen, asshole."

"Alright, I'm through fuckin' around." The combination of a stressful few days and a little too much alcohol in his blood brought out the destructive side of William that he thought was long and buried. He took a swig of a little liquor bottle he had on him and emptied the contents of his pockets. William took off his watch and placed all his items on the old Lincoln that was parked out back. "You tell me the truth or yer gonna get the living shit beat outta you!"

"Oh, now yer gonna whoop my ass? Just put your stuff back in your pocket before I embarrass you."

"That's it," William said to Roger, who was more than happy to fight with him. A few punches back in forth didn't slow them down. William front kicked Roger and sent him back quite a few feet. Roger threw a coffee can that was lying nearby at William It hit him right in the face. William felt his face with his hand and saw the can had hit him hard enough to drawn blood and make his eye start to swell.

"You little son of a bitch!" William said as he punched Roger and pushed him back even further. The two of them continued to exchange blows as their tempers flared and their faces became more and more bruised and bloodied. William was bigger and stronger but the kid was fast, dirty, full of energy and sober.

The sound of engines being redlined could be heard for a mile. The two ignored the sound and kept shoving and punching each other. Both of the exhausted men looked over like a deer in headlights at a police car in the alley slowly coming towards them with lights flashing. The tires screeched to a halt and an officer jumped out of the car with his weapon drawn.

"Both of ya's against the wall now!"

Saturday Afternoon:

"And here I am," William finished to Mitch and Riley who were quite tired of being at the jail.

"Wow, William, I had no idea just how serious things were getting with this track record," Mitch said.

"It really wasn't. I guess I just sorta had enough. I kinda snapped. We hardly beat each other up. We didn't need to be arrested. I wonder who snitched on us?"

"Well," Riley said. "Lucky for you city council hasn't passed that bill that would make public fighting a high misdemeanor with a mandatory jail sentence. It's still just a petty offense if both parties were mutually wanting to fight."

"Yeah he wanted to fight me. In fact he started it."

"Well, you're only giving city council reason to pass stricter laws," Riley continued.

"Be glad we have a city council again," William replied with a smirk.

"What you mean?" Mitch asked.

"Oh, no. No!" Riley replied.

"Well," William started. "At city hall it used to just be Randy Casner at the end of a really long table in a huge room by himself. He would just sit there with all the proposed laws and say 'I approve that, I don't approve that. I approve that, I don't approve that.' Nobody else was ever there to help. He just voted in whatever he wanted by himself."

Mitch laughed and Riley shook his head at William's Randy Casner joke that annoyed him. Even though this was not a serious charge it just wasn't the time or place to be making Casner reference. It seemed to Riley that if the cops had not shown up either Roger or William would have been beat up pretty bad. On the good side, Riley also believed that William just had a bad night and that this would not be the start of some long drawn out meaningless war.

"I do hope this was just a bad night for you," Riley said. "I can't see any reason why you'd do this. Frankly, I think it's due to drinking too much."

"Well, Riley, maybe you should come back when you're sober."

"Oh my God," Riley replied to the idiot joke that Mitch was

cracking up at.

The jailor walked in the check up on them.

"William," Riley said. "The jailor may have been slightly eavesdropping on our conversation. He may be trying to get information or a confession for court."

"No, no," The jailor said. "William just talks too loud and I was just wondering why a local business owner was in here. I'll tell ya, It's a relief from the usual low life drug dealer or DUI."

"Hey," William asked "if what I did was a petty offense, why I am still here?"

"You can leave when you blow zeros through the breathalyzer," the jailor replied.

"Well, I'm feeling pretty aggravated, so I must be sober. Can I blow again?"

"Okay, but I'm not gonna blow you all day. If you don't blow zeros this time you'll have to stay the night again."

William, Mitch and Riley laughed. Riley could tell the jailor didn't even hint that he thought it was funny that he would not "blow him all day." After a quick test of the machine he was ready for William to blow into it. William blew hard until it clicked. All four of them waited in anticipation of where he would be spending the night. After a few seconds the machine indicated William had no alcohol left in his breath.

"Okay, Mr. Defreno, we can get you started through the release process. Do you have a ride home?"

"Uh, do I?" William said to Riley with hope in his face.

"Yeah, I'll take him home," Riley replied.

William was taken to his cell to clean up and then to the release area. He was given his clothes back and signed off that all his belongings were given back. The only part that made him distressed was having to sign his court summons for the petty offense and receive a court date. It didn't look like this would cost a lot of money but would be a pain to go to court during lunch rush.

While the deputies took their sweet time getting everything signed off, William began to daydream brainless thoughts. If someone had to serve a forty year sentence it would be funny when they got their clothes back and they were like plaid bell bottoms or something.

Also, it seemed funny to him that when he had driven by the courthouse at night in the past, the cars still left in the parking lot were probably from people who drove to courthouse and were sentenced to jail.

He wondered if it would be a good idea to have long term parking at the courthouse for people who don't plan to be able to pick up their car for a while. Nervous laughter came from him again as he thought about what would have happened if he had been sentenced to fourteen years back in the day. It was a good thing for him to be able to laugh at such a horrible fate that never came true.

If it had come true the long term parking would have been his only reasonable option when parking for sentencing day. The sentence would be over now, but the Lincoln would be covered in leaves, bird poop, dust, sap and the battery would be dead. Trying to get it started would be problematical with fourteen year old gas and an oxidized engine. The tires would be shot as well and maybe even a window might be broken. What the parking space would look like when he finally moved it made him laugh out loud again.

"You amusing yourself over there? Why are you giggling to yourself?" The jailor asked.

"No, just need to do something to pass the time. If you went any slower you'd be going back in time. If we go back far enough I'll tell myself not to fight with the kid."

"I'm going as fast as I can," The jailor replied.

After an hour of processing, that seemed like five, William got to go through the last door to the waiting area. Even the air smelled better once the final door was opened.

"Here we are, freedom. Don'cha be comin' back here, now," the deputy said as he let William walk his last step to the outside world again. William took a deep breath and smelled some light rain in the air on the warm night.

Chapter 4

Two Front War

While William sat in jail Ralph stood alone in the kitchen of Andrea's house carefully picking through the garbage. A greasy smile oozed across his lips as he found what he was looking for. He crossed to the sink and dropped the cap from one of the boys' chocolate milk bottles down the drain. He added a few pieces of orange peel for good measure. Outside, he heard the sound of Andrea's car pulling up.

"Just in time," he muttered under his breath.

He watched as she pulled two large paper sacks full of groceries and a heavy bag of potatoes out of the trunk and struggled to carry them up the walk. When she was about two thirds of the way to the house he hurried out to meet her.

"Here, let me help," said Ralph, taking one of the bags and the sack of potatoes.

"Whew, thanks," said Andrea. "I was about to drop them, and I have eggs in there."

"Can't have that, now. Eggs are expensive." Ralph pulled the screen door open with his foot. "After you."

Andrea and Ralph set the groceries on the table. Andrea started putting things away in the fridge.

"That's quite a haul," said Ralph. "We expecting an army for dinner, or just Geoff and William again?"

"William won't be here. Saturday's are busy at the diner. He'll probably be working til after midnight.

"Aw, that's too bad."

Andrea shrugged. "it's not his fault."

"Still sucks."

Andrea continued putting groceries away. She got frustrated by a pantry door that at first wouldn't open, and then wouldn't close.

"This damn house!" she yelled as she slammed the door again to try to force it shut.

Ralph came up beside her. "It has its quirks, that's for sure." He took a look at the door. "It needs planing. I could do it for you tomorrow. Uh, unless William would mind."

"Why would he mind?"

"I don't know. Maybe it's just me, but whenever I have a girlfriend I kinda take pride in making sure I take care of everything she needs around the house. I don't like another guy messing with it."

"Trust me, William won't mind. He has too much to do as it is."

"He seems to always find time to eat and smoke, though."

Andrea crossed over to the sink. Like he knew she would if he made her nervous, she started to fill herself a glass of water. She noticed the sink wasn't draining.

"Oh, great." Andrea headed for the laundry room and came back with a tool box. She opened the lid and took out a wrench.

"Can't you call somebody to do that?"

"Plumbers are expensive."

"What about Geoff, or your dad? I mean since you're boyfriend's too busy to help you."

"I'm a big girl. I can do my own household chores."

Ralph took the wrench. "Of course you can, but you shouldn't have to. You do way too much by yourself as it is."

He opened the cupboard under the sink. In just a few minutes he had the pipe apart and had knocked the bottle cap and peels loose. Then he put the sink parts back together. While his hands were out of sight he deliberately pinched his index finger with the wrench. Blood welled up from the wound.

"Ouch!" he yelped.

"Oh no! What happened?"

"It's nothing." Ralph wound a paper towel around his injured finger.

"Let me look."

Ralph held out his hand. Andrea peeked under the towel. "Ooh," she said. "Let me take care of that."

She got the first aid kit out, cleaned Ralph's cut and put a bandage on it.

"You are one impressive lady, you know that," said Ralph.

Andrea blushed. "What makes you say that?"

"Just everything. You work all day, manage the house, cook, clean, help your sister with her kids, look after of all us big dumb guys and still find time to draw flowers."

"How did you know about that?"

Ralph took Andrea's sketch book out of his pocket. "You left it on the porch."

"Oh."

Ralph flipped through the book. "How come you never show anybody these?"

"I don't know, just shy I guess."

"You should, though. They're really good."

"You think so?"

"Yeah, yeah, I really do. People really need to see how talented you are."

"I don't know. I mean they're kinda private."

"Well what about William? You could show him, right?"

"I guess. It's just, well..."

"What?"

"What if he thinks they're silly?"

"He won't think that. Not if he really cares about you."

"Um, okay. I guess maybe I'll show him."

"Good for you."

Riley pulled up behind the diner. William hopped out of the car. Mitch and Riley followed him into his small house at the back of the property.

"We gotta hurry," Riley said. "We opened for dinner almost an hour ago."

"The staff can handle it for a little longer," said William. He ducked into his bathroom for a quick shower. He came out a few minutes later with his hair still dripping and pulled on a fresh shirt. Riley checked his watch again.

"Riley, relax. We pay those people good money. They know their jobs."

"We still ought to be there."

"We will be... in a minute." William reached for a whiskey bottle and three glasses.

"William!"

"Riley, if I wanted an uptight old lady running my diner I'd have hired your mom. Now will you please chill? We need this."

"It has been a long day," said Mitch. He settled down in a chair near the door. "Been a long time since we were this stressed out about something."

"Maybe since you were," said Riley. "Running a restaurant isn't exactly a low stress occupation."

"You think being an LPN is? You know what I go through each day?"

"How long before you get your R.N.?" William asked as he handed Mitch a glass of whiskey. He passed a second glass to Riley before picking up his own.

"Forever," answered Mitch. "I've been taking classes for six years now and I'm still not done."

"Why is it taking you so long?" asked Riley.

"I'm taking the classes a few at a time so I don't get overloaded. Man, I don't know how some people go to school full time and work full time. I'm maxed out at half a course load."

"You just need to apply yourself more," said Riley.

"Look who's talking! You spent four years on a Bachelor's degree in science and another five getting your Master's in engineering and here you are working for William."

Riley shook his head. "Funny, isn't it? All I wanted was to make a better world. I had this idea for a car engine that would get a hundred miles to a gallon of gas. I figured it was a gold mine. Then I got out there and found out nobody wants a better world. They just want to find bigger and better ways to blow up the one we've already got."

"Wow," said William.

"It's true. All the best government grants go for weapons research."

"So now what are you gonna do?" asked Mitch.

"Build it anyway," said Riley. "Soon as William and I make

enough off this place for me to build a lab."

"Just be careful someone doesn't mistake you for the town's new meth distributor," said William

"Ha ha," Riley said with a sarcastic tone.

"You should teach, Riley," said Mitch. "You'd make an awesome teacher."

Riley looked shocked. "Are you serious?"

"Why not?" said William. "You'd be way better than the teachers we had. They sucked."

"Like Mrs. Wilson?" Mitch made a sour face. "She was such a bitch."

"Exactly," said William. "She treated us like we were a bunch losers and dumb asses, but here we are, Riley's got a master's degree, you're a nurse and I'm a restaurant owner. One day Moe's diner is gonna be a franchise I'll make it so good."

"You know you're right," Mitch said. "Look at all the little spoiled brat kids she treated so well. You know how many of them still live at home in their thirties, drunk and unemployed?"

"Yeah," Riley said. "She didn't have the vision to see that people who have to work for what they get and don't get it handed to them often do better than those who have a charmed life."

"Do you guys remember when we brought her down to the hospital and pretended her son needed blood?" Mitch asked.

"Yeah, how could I forget," William said.

"Oh my God," Riley added as he put his face in his hand. "I still can't believe we got away with that."

"What do ya think ever happened to that hot teacher Ms. Hank?" William asked.

"Probably works at private club a few blocks from," Riley replied.

"Oh you mean The Love House?" said Mitch

"Yeah, I bet you know all about that place, huh Mitch?"

"Hey Riley, I swear I was just there to get direction on how to get out of there."

"Uh-huh."

The sound of several loud crashes suddenly came from the diner.

"Looks like our little trip down memory lane's over," said Riley.

"We better get over there."

"Right behind you," said William, though whatever was happening, he wasn't sure he wanted to know about it.

"Hey, what about me? My car's still at the hospital!" said Mitch.

Riley and William looked at each other.

"We could have him wait tables," said William.

"Dressed like that? Nah, we'd better put him to work in the kitchen."

"Maybe." They could now hear the sounds of an argument coming from the diner's kitchen. "Sounds like we're about to fire a dishwasher."

"Oh very funny, guys," said Mitch. "Come on, I gotta work in the morning."

"Relax, we'll call you a cab," said William.

"Gee, thanks."

Back at Andrea's, Shelly sat on the porch while she watched her boys play in the yard. Phillip and Thomas ran back and forth screaming as they kicked a blue and white soccer ball up and down the lawn. Every few minutes she tried to turn her attention back to the brochure in her lap, but she couldn't seem to concentrate on it.

Ralph came out and sat down beside her. She scooted over a little on the bench to make room.

"Sure is a pretty night, huh?" said Ralph.

"Yeah, it's nice."

"Too nice for a pretty girl to be wearing such a serious frown."

Shelly looked down at her shoes. "Thanks."

Ralph reached up and tucked a lock of Shelly's hair behind her ear. His hand lingered on her cheek. "You should tie your hair back more. Let everyone see those gorgeous eyes of yours."

"No one notices my eyes."

"They will if you stop hiding them behind all that hair."

"Maybe." Shelly moved again. The brochure fell out of her lap and hit the ground. Ralph picked it up.

"What's this?" he asked.

"Oh, that's nothing," Shelly said. She reached to take it back but Ralph pulled it away. He held the brochure up to the porch light to get a better look.

"Centurion Dental College, huh?"

Shelly bit her lip. "Yeah. I keep seeing their commercials on TV so I thought I'd check them out. Time's moving so fast. Phillip's already going to be in fourth grade next year and I'm not sending the boys to college on what I make at the pet store."

"True," Ralph conceded. "So why are you hesitating?"

"It's just a lot to take on, with work and the boys, and it's expensive. Tuition's like ten thousand dollars for a nine month program."

"Bet you could find a way to come up with that."

"Well, I could ask my dad, I guess."

"Oh?" said Ralph. "I never realized he had that kind of money."

Shelly laughed. "No one does. He keeps it that way on purpose. But he's actually pretty well off. He bought a lot of the right stocks at the right times. He's always been lucky like that."

"Well then, I'm sure he'll be glad to help you pay for school."

"It's a lot of work, though. Especially the math. I hate math."

"I'll help with that. There's a lot of math in construction, you know."

"I bet." Shelly took a deep breath. "You really think I could do it?"

"Honey, you could do anything."

Shelly beamed a smile.

Sunday morning dawned bright and already warm. William woke up late and took his time getting up. He pulled on his bathrobe, made himself coffee and eggs and was just considering a batch of pancakes when Riley knocked on the door.

"Remind me to move," said William.

"Good morning to you, too," said Riley. "You planning on coming to work?"

William paused for a moment. The silence stretched on and on.

"Well?" said Riley.

"I'm thinking about it," said William.

"Think about this; there's a delivery driver out here demanding payment for an order of five hundred pounds of goat meat and two hundred pounds of ostrich. And he insists on talking to the owner, so you better put some pants on and get out here." With that Riley went back to the diner, leaving William's front door open.

"Great," said William. He pulled on a pair of jeans and a t-shirt. As he laced up his sneakers he wondered how this mix up happened. Maybe the guy had the wrong restaurant, or maybe it was something the crazy chef they'd fired last month had set up before he left. Either way, William figured it was going to be a headache to deal with. Goat was expensive. He didn't know anything about ostrich meat but he suspected it was pretty pricey, too. Thinking about it, William realized he wasn't even sure if ostrich meat was legal.

The large, muscular, very pissed off looking driver stood leaning against he cab of his truck. "You Defreno?" he asked.

"Yeah, that's me," said William.

The guy held out a clipboard. "Sign here. And I'll need a check for three-thousand four hundred and twenty-eight dollars."

"Now hang on," said William. "There's been some kind of mistake. I didn't order this meat."

"Yeah, well I got a purchase order that says you did."

"Let me see that." William took the clip board. "This isn't my tax I.D. number. And you don't even have my name spelled right."

"So our secretary can't type. We'll hire another one soon as I get that check."

"No check. This is not my order."

"Oh yeah?"

"Yeah."

"We'll see about that, buddy."

"Yes we will. Get your boss on the phone."

"My boss is a busy man, you know."

"So am I. Either you call him or my lawyer can. Which is it?"

"Alright, alright." the driver pulled out an old fashioned flip style cell phone and dialed a number. "Hey Lou, it's Greg. Yeah, I'm trying to deliver this meat but the guy here says he didn't order it. He wants to talk to you." Greg paused for a moment and listened as someone on the other end of the line replied. "Uh huh, yeah, hang on."

Greg held out the phone. William took it. "I'm Sorry about the confusion. This is William Defreno at Moe's Diner and I'm telling you we did not place this order. You don't even have our business details right on the form."

"Oh well you'd have talk to Joe in purchasing about that," said the deep, rough voice that William could only assume was Lou.

"Well let me talk to Joe, then."

"Hang on." There was a series of clicks and some buzzing on the line. Then he heard Lou bellowing. "Hey, Joe, line two!"

"Jesus," muttered William.

A moment later another voice came on the line. "This is Joe in purchasing. How can I help you today, sir?"

William sighed and explained for the third time that not he, nor anyone else associated with Moe's Diner, had every ordered either goat or ostrich meat.

"Let me check the system," said Joe. William could hear him typing rapidly on a keyboard.

"Moe's Diner. Yeah, we got the order yesterday. Rush delivery. You're saying you didn't order this?"

"No, I didn't."

"So you're saying you're not William Defreno?"

"I am not saying that."

"Then you're saying that's not Moe's Diner?"

"No, I'm not saying that, either!"

"Then what are you saying, sir?"

"I'm saying I didn't order ostrich meat! Until this morning I didn't know it was even possible to order ostrich meat."

"Oh, so you just ordered the goat, then?"

"No, I did not order goat meat!"

"Sir, I'm confused."

William muffled a scream. "Alright," he said. "I'm going to make this very simple for you. I did not order any of this meat. I do not want this meat and I am not paying for this meat. Now get your driver and his truck out of here pronto or I'm going to sue you, your buddy Lou and your driver here for fraud and extortion. Is that clear enough?"

"Perfectly clear, sir. Sorry for the confusion."

Joe hung up. William handed the driver his phone. "You heard that. Now beat it."

"Alright, I'm goin'. Geez, what an asshole!"

Greg climbed into the truck of his cab and took off.

William went into the diner. Goat meat! What next?

The phone rang. William answered it automatically.

"Yeah, can I get two goat meat burritos and an ostrich burger to go?" The question was followed by hysterical laughter. William slammed down the phone. Though the caller had tried to disguise his voice, William recognized it pretty easily.

"See if you can find a number for Roger or his parents," he told Riley. "Looks like he was behind this little incident."

It turned out Roger's family was actually listed in the local phone book. After a brief debate they decided it might be better if Riley called. Roger wasn't home but Riley talked to the boy's mother.

"Ma'am, I understand that Roger's already in some trouble. We don't want to make it any worse, but what he did was pretty serious. He needs to come down here to straighten it out or we'll have to call the police."

"Oh God, please don't do that! His father will kill me!"

"We won't have to, Ma'am, just as long as you get him down here in the next half hour."

"Okay. I'll see what I can do."

They didn't have to wait long. Roger's mother dropped him off in front of the diner within ten minutes. Riley and William met him at the door and escorted him over to the bar. They sat down on stools on either side of Roger, squashing him between them.

"So, ostrich meat, huh?" William started.

"What'cha talkin' about?"

"Come on kid," Riley added. "If you're gonna play a prank on someone don't call them and confess to it. And even if you are that stupid, don't call from your home phone. The diner has caller I.D."

"I'm not that stupid. I called from a payphone."

"So you did call," said William. "And since only the guy who ordered the meat could make that call it means you did that, too."

"Man!" said Roger. "That's entrapment! You tricked me!"

"We aren't in court, kid," said Riley. "And William and I aren't cops. We're just three guys talking."

"Looks more like two bullies picking on a kid to me," said Roger.

"And leave my mom alone!"

"Hey, lose the attitude, and stop playing games. You didn't break the record. Even if you did it wasn't verified. You need to stop blaming others for your short comings."

"Also," William added. "I heard you've been busted for pot a few times."

"Yeah, so what?"

"Here, look at this," William said as he handed Roger a piece of paper.

"What?" Roger asked as grabbed the paper with both hands and noticed it was blank.

"Oh, wait, I meant this," William said as he took the blank piece of paper away and handed him a pamphlet on the dangers of marijuana.

"Oh, where'd you get this?"

"From the New Laws program. I donate a lot of money to them in order to stop kids from being criminals."

"Oh my God, you mean those three bozos who go from school to school screaming at the kids?"

"Hey, they have good numbers that show their program works, maybe you should listen to them."

"Maybe you guys should come see those fools in action. They don't prevent shit. You're wasting your money."

"Anyway, they're trying help," Riley added. "So are we. If you don't wanna get in anymore trouble you leave us and this diner alone. You get my drift?"

"Yeah, fine. Just don't call my mom again, okay?"

"Keep your nose clean and we won't. Now beat it."

"Whatever. Smell you later, assholes."

Roger stalked out of the diner.

At Andrea's house, she, Geoff, Shelly and Ralph sat lingering over their coffee while the boys watched cartoons on the living room floor.

"Dad called me last night," said Geoff.

"What'd he want?" asked Andrea.

"Looks like he's finally going to repair the hot tub room. He wanted me to come help him put up drywall."

"About time," said Shelly. "I was really starting to worry about the mold in there."

"I know. The thing is he wants to do it Thursday, and I'm already gonna be gone."

"Oh, that's right!" said Andrea. "You'll be in Cincinnati."

"Yeah. I mean I feel awful 'cause you know I'd do anything for dad, but I've had a ticket to this convention for like a year and my hotel room's non-refundable."

"Did you tell him?"

"Yeah. He said he understood, but he sounded really disappointed."

"Oh."

"I can help," said Ralph. "I'm not doing much good just sitting around here."

"Would you?" said Andrea. "That would be great! We'd really appreciate it."

"Glad to do it. It's the least I can do with how great you guys have been to me. Besides, I remember that I liked your dad as a kid."

"I'll call him right now." Shelly said. She threw her arms around Ralph and hugged him tight. "You're the best!"

"No, you are."

"Yeah, thanks Ralph," said Geoff. He sounded a lot less enthusiastic about the idea than the girls.

"No problem, buddy." Ralph slapped Geoff on the back. "You just go enjoy playing with your balls."

Ralph laughed to himself as he walked out of the room.

After a busy, but highly successful, lunch shift William and Riley sat down in the diner's office to go over the books like they did every Sunday. Even after paying all the month's bills and William's generous donations there was still plenty of money in the checking account.

"That is an impressive total," said Riley.

"Think of how much higher it would be if I wasn't making all these donations," said William. He waved a stack donation receipts around to prove the point.

"Yeah, but you're basically a new business. Not too bad of an idea to get the city on your side and make a few friends in the community."

"Good friends aren't cheap."

"It's worth it, though. Besides a lot of the things you donate to you actually like. And they listened to you at the school because you're paying the bills of the track team."

"True. I do really like the New Laws program. I mean what better way to stop criminals than go to the schools when they're young and let them know what can happen to them and what they can do better?"

"I've heard a lot of good things about those guys. They even go to the elementary school and talk to them about drugs crime and such."

"They say it really helps and it's not cheese ball like that D.A.R.E. program we had when we were in school."

"Maybe those guys need to pay a visit to Roger's classroom when he goes back to school in September."

"Yeah, they can tell him what happens when you lie about breaking a track record."

"You never know. Roger's probably a lost cause, but there are other kids it might help." Riley paused for a moment then looked at William with a puzzled expression. "You know, I think all your donations got you some special treatment in jail, too. I mean, I don't believe in bribing the city, but helping out should get returns. It's probably the reason the burlesque house has no trouble staying open."

"Oh yeah, the ol' Love House. I know what you mean. I heard it's basically a whore house."

"Yeah that's the one. It's actually pretty classy, but without them making generous donations to the city I think they'd be under fire."

"You ever been there, Riley?"

"Yeah, Mitch made me go with him."

"Oh, he made you?"

"Well, it was his idea. I'm pretty sure the owner donated thousands to the new jail project. I bet he would get treated well if they ever busted him."

"Yeah, well I donated more than I could afford to help the new jail expansion, they better treat me well. I probably paid that deputy's salary."

William's cell phone lit up. He checked the screen and saw a text message from Andrea.

"U coming for dinner?" it read. "Making pot roast & mashed potatoes."

"Andrea?" asked Riley.

"Yeah. She's making dinner. Do you mind? I know I've left you on your own a lot lately."

"Nah. Sunday night's pretty slow anyway."

"Thanks. See you later."

"See ya."

Andrea was just setting the table when William arrived carrying two fresh apple pies from the diner.

"Those smell great," she said as she took them into the kitchen.

William headed into the dining room. He noticed the house was really quiet. Through the window he spotted Shelly and the boys out back with Ralph. He was taking turns teaching them karate kicks.

"Oh, great, that's just what they need," William muttered. He leaned against the doorway to the kitchen, shaking his head as he watched the boys learn better ways to kill each other. After a few minutes Ralph said something to Shelly. She hurried into house, ducking under the arm William had stretched out across the kitchen doorway. A moment later she returned with a glass of lemonade.

"God, will you get out of my way?" she said to William as she ducked under his arm again.

"What the-" William said, but Shelly was already out in the yard handing Ralph his drink before William could finish the thought.

Geoff came in behind William. He carried three two liter bottles of soda and a six pack of beer.

"Hey, what's going on?" he asked.

"Take a look," said William. He jerked his head towards the window.

"Huh. That doesn't look anything like the stuff I learned in karate class."

"Really? Something about it looks familiar, though."

Geoff watched carefully for another moment or two. "Well, I

can't say for sure," said he. "But I think I saw that move on an episode of Power Rangers."

Dinner was finally ready. Andrea called everyone in and they settled around the dining table. Grass and mud from the boys' antics still streaked their clothes and hair. No one told them to wash up.

William sat across Ralph. At first William thought Ralph was staring at him, then he realized Ralph was actually staring out the window. William turned around and saw what had caught Ralph's attention. The hot young blond next door was out in her yard, bending over in tight shorts as she trimmed the flower bushes in front of her house.

"Hey Andrea." said Ralph. "Who's that hot chick next door?"

"Oh, that's Julie," Andrea said. I don't know much about her. She just moved in a few weeks ago."

"Geoff's talked to her," said Shelly. "You asked her out, didn't you Geoff?"

"Yes, I did. Forget it buddy," Geoff said to Ralph. "She lives with a six foot three body builder."

"Oh yeah?" said Ralph. "Well someone better tell that guy to stay away from my new girlfriend." He growled quietly to himself as he watched the blond walk up her front steps.

"So how's that job going?" William asked Ralph.

"Oh man, they delayed me. But I told 'em if they wanted me to stay on I need to get back pay. So I'm technically getting paid to do nothing until I start."

"How do you afford anything until yer check comes?"

"Well Andrea's been helping me, but she won't regret it. I guess now is a good time to tell you. When I get my first check I'm gonna buy a new furnace for the house."

"You don't have to do that, Ralph. You've been very helpful around the house and with the kids." Andrea said.

"Na, I want to. I know it costs a lot to convert boiler to forced air, but I don't care. Just find someone whose competent and I'm gonna pay for the whole thing cause you've been so good to me."

"He's gonna help dad with his house will Geoff's gone, too," said Shelly.

"Oh really?" William looked from Ralph to Geoff. Was he

imagining it, or was Geoff looking a little unhappy about that?

"What can I say, I'm just that kind of guy." Ralph dug into his pot roast. William looked down at his plate. Suddenly he didn't feel very hungry.

After dinner William and Andrea went out to the back deck to smoke and have a few drinks. It was the first real time they'd had to spend together in days.

"I have something I want to show you," said Andrea. She took her sketchbook out and handed to William.

"What's this?" He asked.

"Oh, you know, just some pictures I drew of the yard and the garden and stuff."

"Cool." He set it down next to his glass.

"Don't you want to look at it?"

"Maybe later."

"Oh." Andrea looked disappointed. William smiled at her.

"Right now all I want to look at is you."

"Oh," she said again, this time sounding much happier. She poured them both another drink. William gave her a questioning look. She explained. "I don't have to work tomorrow."

"I see." He pulled her close. "Maybe I'll just stay here tonight, then."

"I'd like that."

"So would I."

Despite the late hour, though, they could not get any privacy. The boys, being on summer break and fueled up by all the sugary soda they'd had with dinner were still tearing through the house like manic squirrels. Ralph kept wandering by, laughing out loud at the videos he was watching on his tablet. Then Shelly came out to talk about some fly-by-night dental school she wanted to enroll in. William had heard of the place. Half his waitstaff had gone there and now had hefty tuition bills but no dental jobs to pay them. William wondered if he should tell Shelly the place was a scam. Before he could though, her cell phone rang. Even from five feet away he could hear Melissa's grating voice on the other end. Instead of going back inside, Shelly sat with them to take the call, which seemed to go on forever.

Finally William gave up and went to bed. He fell asleep before Andrea came up to join him.

Chapter 5

For Whom the Bell Tolls

In the morning, William awoke to the sounds of the boys running through the house yelling and fighting. With a loud moan, he pulled a pillow over his head and tried to go back to sleep. Soon, though, the smells of fresh coffee and bacon frying coaxed him out of bed.

Down in the kitchen the girls were laughing and talking as they put bacon, eggs, and pancakes on large platters to serve at the table. When he saw Shelly, William vaguely remembered wanting to tell her something, but he could not remember what it was. Instead he mumbled "good morning" and reached for the coffee pot.

In the dining room, Ralph sat at the table. Every muscle was tensed as he stared out the window. He seemed to be waiting for something. Coffee in hand, William wandered over to join him. They watched as the blond next door came out her front door. She took a note off her windshield, read it, and then looked over at Andrea's house with a confused expression.

"Here we go," said Ralph. "Control, we have lift off!" He got more and more excited as she approached the house. He jumped up and opened the front door before she could even knock.

"Hi," The skinny blond twenty year old neighbor girl said. She still had the puzzled look on her smooth, pretty face. William could see Ralph was instantly turned on by her ample chest and model-like body.

"I got this note to come over here and see Ralph as soon as possible," she said in her soft feminine voice.

"Yeah, that's me," Ralph said. "I'm new in town and until my two hundred grand a year job starts I been just keeping this place nice. In the meantime, I assigned myself neighborhood patrol. I used to do patrol in the special forces. This morning I was playing my guitar outside- I'm a musician ya know- I looked over at your house and I saw the biggest Mexican you'd even seen. I mean big as shit!" Ralph said as he threw his hands up and to the side to illustrate how big this guy was.

"Oh," she replied.

"Yeah, I mean big and dark. I don't mean his skin or the fact he dressed in all black and chains. I mean it was like he was always walking in a shadow. Like the sunlight just sorta got out of his way. You never could see the creep's face. Anyway, he pulled out a slimjim and tried to break into your car. In a few seconds he had popped the door and I saw him take your CD case," Ralph said and showed he had the CD case that was in her car.

"Oh my," she replied.

"Well, I wouldn't allow it. I went up to this guy and said you ain't taking that CD case or her car without gettin' past me," Ralph continued nodding his head and taking a moment of silence for effect. "He handed it to me and ran off screaming. Haven't seen him since," Ralph continued as he handed her the CD case back.

"Oh, how terrible. I don't know what to say," She replied in skepticism.

"Well, no thanks is necessary. Just doing my job. You're welcome to come here anytime you have any problems or for any reason you want."

"Okay."

"I mean it, you name the vice, I'll name the price. Of course, anything is always free for you."

"Okay," she repeated.

"You'll be seeing a lot of me around here. That motorcycle out front is mine. Me and my boys go ridin' all the time."

"Cool, I'll see you. Thanks, I guess," She replied uneasily. She left and Ralph continued to go on and on about the huge dark Mexican.

"Slam dunk, she's mine!" Ralph said to William. William had his doubts, but didn't feel like saying so. He had just sat down with his coffee when Melissa walked in without knocking.

"Hey Mel," said Shelly. "What are you doing here?"

"I need Andrea to drive me to the mall. Mommy gave me money for new jeans."

"That's like an hour away," said William. "Can't you just go to the outlet store downtown?"

"My skin's too sensitive to wear knockoffs." Mel helped herself to a plate of bacon and eggs.

"Want some coffee with that?" Andrea asked her.

"What kind do you have?"

"Just Folgers."

"Ew. How come you buy that junk? Why don't you ever buy good coffee?"

"Folgers is great. We serve it at the diner," said William.

"That's why you're going out of business. Everybody knows the only good coffee is Starbucks. That's why so many businesses have one. Maybe you should open one in the diner."

"You think I should open a Starbucks in the diner?"

"At least then you might make some money and buy Andrea some nice stuff. She doesn't have any nice stuff. You don't buy her any."

"Andrea can buy her own stuff."

"Then what does she need you for?"

William had had enough. "I gotta go," he said. He pulled Andrea into a hug from behind and kissed her neck. "Wanna come by the diner for lunch later?"

"She doesn't want to eat your crappy food, William," said Melissa. "I want McDonald's for lunch. We can get that at the mall."

"I'll take you to the mall if you want," said Ralph.

"I'm not going to the mall with you on your stupid bike. Everyone will think I'm a loser."

"You used to love to ride on my bike."

"No, I didn't. I always thought it was dumb. I was just trying to be nice. You're bike's the crappiest piece of shit ever. Besides Andrea needs to go to the mall. All her clothes are ugly. She needs new clothes."

"Have fun," William said to Andrea as he left. He had just reached his car when she called him back.

"You forgot this," she said. She handed him her sketchbook.

"Oh, right. I'll have a look later." He tossed it in the back seat and took off.

Riley was waiting for William at the front door of the diner. It was apparent by the look on Riley's face that another horrible thing had happened. William's mind began to consider many possibilities. Was the staff freaking out, a customer getting food poisoning, Ralph doing something, Roger up to no good or even the Casners back for round three? Rather than draw out the suspense he let out a sigh, shook his head and approached Riley.

"Alright, William, calm down," Riley said.

"Calm down? I haven't said one word. I don't even know what's going on."

"Just calm down."

"What? What is it?"

"The diner's website has been hacked. We're trying to fix it, but we might get a few nasty phone calls until it's back to normal."

"Oh Jesus God! Let me see it."

William went to Moesdiner.com and saw what uncalled for nonsense had been done to him this time. The headline now said "Welcome to Moe's crappy Diner, serving the best dog in the world."

"Oh man," William moaned.

He just shook his head continued reading the new menu. "Come enjoy barbecued dog, boiled dog, broiled dog, baked dog, sautéed dog, dog kabobs, dog gumbo, deep fried dog, stir-fried dog, dog soup, dog salad, and dog sandwich. Oh and if your dog is missing we don't know where he is."

William looked at the illustrations on the menu that used to have pictures of food, but instead now had pictures of dogs with the prices and availability of each dog. There was everything from pugs at market price to rack of dachshund ribs to poodles stew. Even dog catering was available for birthdays, weddings, and graduations. The Moe's Diner biography had been changed, too.

"At Moe's Diner we don't run things well. Most of our staff can't run at all. Any time another restaurant runs better or wins an award we just pay off the authorities to take it away. We do weird things to your food and donate money to the New Laws program that makes kids start hating cops at a young age and creates more crime in the city. However, we love criminals at Moe's Diner. In fact we're owned by the biggest criminal in town. Just check out these links."

William clicked one of the links. An old newspaper article came up titled, "William Defreno Gets The Big One." Another link brought up an article that was titled, "William Defreno Strikes Again."

"Wow, did he really have to dig up all the trouble from my past and put it on display like that?" William said.

"Ya know, too bad this kid couldn't use his creativity to like write a funny book or something instead of doing things like this." Riley stated.

"Yeah, it's stupid. When will the real website be up and running?"

"The tech guys said hopefully by the end of the day."

"'Til then we're just screwed?"

"Pretty much. I called the cops, even though you hate them. They don't have a computer crimes unit. Without a confession they can't prove it was him."

"Figures. I didn't think they would."

"I could try the FBI, but I don't know if they would consider this serious enough."

"Do I donate money to the FBI?"

"I don't think so, William."

"Then forget it! They'll probably laugh."

William was already on his last nerve from dealing with the drama at Andrea's that morning. He went behind the bar and threw a beer mug on the ground. The loud crash of shattering glass startled Riley. A couple eating in the dining area heard it as well.

"William, we have customers in the dining room," Riley said.

"I don't care, man. I can't believe he had to post my newspapers articles. What if people in town see them? I was pretty sure everyone here had forgotten who I was and what I did. Now, that could open up a whole can of worms."

"I don't know. It'll be gone in a few hours."

The telephone rang and William answered it.

"Moe's Diner."

"I find it very offensive that you cook dogs. I'm calling the humane society." an elderly voice said.

"Are you fuckin' stupid lady? Do you really think we cook dogs?"

Riley snatched the phone out of William's hand.

"Ma'am, this is Riley, I'm the manger here. Our website was hacked. We do not cook dogs here at Moe's Diner, nor do we endorse animal cruelty of any kind. Within a few hours our real site should be back up and running. I hope you will come visit us and see what we have to offer."

After a minute Riley was done talking to the concerned customer on the phone.

"Man, it pisses me off," William said as he threw another mug on the ground.

"William, could you like work in the back and not answer the phone till you calm down?"

"Sure."

William pulled a bucket, mop, scrub brush and sponges out of the supply closet. He filled the bucket with soap and hot, steaming water. He opened the walk in cooler and started scrubbing. It was too quiet, though. He could still hear himself think. Frustrated, he threw the sponge into the bucket and left the cooler. He came back with a radio, found a classic rock station and turned it up as loud as it would go. That was better.

He cleaned in tune with the music. As he scrubbed, he sang along to the lyrics, loudly and badly, not caring who could hear him. While he worked, ideas for various revenge fantasies played out in his head. He imagined the spots on the walls and floor were Roger hiding in the jungle and the steaming water he dropped on them was napalm. He mimicked agonized screams as the targets were obliterated. Yeah, Roger was goin' *down*.

"Fire!" sang William, "I'll teach you to bur-rr-rn!"

Nah, burning was too good for the little fucker. But something had to be done. Getting even with Roger was a moral imperative.

Just then the opening notes of Metallica's "For Whom the Bell Tolls" rolled out of the radio's speakers. William looked at the radio in shock. Metallica was definitely classic, but even though it was one of their older songs it pained him to hear one of the bands' he listened to in high school playing on an "oldies" station.

It gave him pause to think, though. He was a thirty year old business owner, and here he was standing in the cooler playing kids' games with a sponge and a bucket. It was almost like being Rip Van Winkle; like his teenage self had blinked and then he'd opened his eyes to find himself standing 14 years into the future, not having changed inside, but his body and the world around him having grown older without him knowing it.

Well, if the future was here, he needed to step forward and join it. He had worked too hard and too long to lose everything again in another drawn-out, pointless war. He thought of his secret weapon, the sheet of blank paper tucked safely away in its hiding place. It was time to end this. The bell was tolling, and it tolled for Roger...

Andrea pulled her car into her driveway and set the parking brake. Melissa sat in the passenger seat beside her, still talking about an incident from earlier.

"I don't know what's wrong with those people," said Mel. "They make all their clothes the wrong sizes. I'm a size 5. I've been a size 5 since high school. That dress should have fit. And that sales girl was rude. And stupid. She should know better than to talk to people that way. That whole mall is stupid. I don't know why you go there, anyway."

"It'll be okay, Mel," said Andrea. "The other dress you found was prettier, anyway."

"Yeah, but they should have given me a discount after that other one. I'm gonna call the manager. You just watch."

Mel opened the car door, gathered up her half dozen shopping bags and headed for the house. Andrea got out as well. She closed her door, went around to close the passenger door Mel had left open, and then went into the house.

Ralph sat on the living room couch watching rock videos on TV. He smiled when he saw Andrea.

"Hey, how was the mall?"

"Stupid," said Mel. "They didn't have the right sizes."

"Omar the tent maker went out of business, huh?"

"Shut up! I don't need a tent maker. I'm a size 5."

Ralph looked at her critically. "Don't you mean fifty-five?"

"Screw you, Ralph."

Melissa stormed off into the kitchen.

"Sorry about that," said Andrea. "Mel's a little difficult sometimes."

Ralph waved away the apology. "No need to tell me. I've known her longer than you have. I know how she gets."

"Yeah, you do. Sorry. I guess I'm just used to having to explain for her."

"Why?"

Andrea shrugged. "People don't always understand Mel. She rubs them the wrong way sometimes."

"Never apologize for your friends," said Ralph. "Anyone who accepts you needs to accept them, too. If someone says they don't like your friends they're really saying they think you're stupid or don't trust your judgment. Don't ever let anyone disrespect you like that."

"Huh. I never thought of it like that."

"Most people don't. You gotta look for the hidden meanings in stuff. They taught me that in the service. Intelligence work, you know."

"That must have been interesting."

"Best time of my life. Trouble is if I talk about it they'll shoot me."

"Oh," said Andrea.

"Yeah. We better change the subject. What did William think of your pictures?"

"Well, I gave them to him."

"But?" Ralph looked at her expectantly.

"He didn't look at them."

"Ah." Ralph said sadly. "I wonder what the hidden meaning is in *that*."

"He's just busy. He has a lot on his mind. He'll look when he gets the time."

"I sure hope you're right about that, baby doll." Ralph shook his head. "I sure hope you're right."

William stood alone at the old stove in the diner's kitchen making orders while the cook took his break. He flipped burgers and watched steam rise from a batch of onions browning slowly on his right. He felt calmer than he had before, but still antsy. Now that he finally had a plan he was eager to put it into place.

His phone rang. He almost ignored it, then saw Andrea's name on the caller I.D.

"Hi hon, what's up?"

"Oh not much," said Andrea. "Just wondering if you were coming over for dinner tonight."

William paused. He always wanted to see Andrea, but a houseful of Ralph and the boys was a little more than he thought he wanted to deal with after the day he'd had, especially if Melissa was going to be there. It sounded like she would be. He could hear her loud voice in the background. Geez, didn't she ever go home?

Plus, if he went over there he'd have to wait another whole day before he could do what he needed to in order to end the war with Roger, and who knew what the kid might pull next?

"Honey? Are you there?" Andrea said.

"Sorry," said William. "Just got lost in thought for a second. I'd like to come over for dinner, but I don't think I can. We have a late produce order coming and I have to be here to sign for it."

"Oh." She sounded disappointed.

"I will be there tomorrow night, though, I promise. Can't miss Geoff's big send off."

"Okay, I'll see you then."

"See you then."

She hung up without saying goodbye.

Ralph stood in the kitchen doorway watching Andrea as she hung up the phone.

"Not coming, huh?" he asked.

"Nope. Some sort of diner drama."

Ralph shrugged. "Life happens."

"I guess."

He crossed the room. Taking her chin, he titled her head up to look her right in the eye.

"You need to get out of here for awhile," he said.

"I can't. There's dinner, and the laundry and these papers William

71

gave me about putting me on his health insurance plan..."

"It can wait."

"But-"

"It. Can. Wait." Ralph repeated. He gently steered her out of the kitchen and towards the stairs. "Go put on something pretty. I'm taking you out."

"Ralph-" Andrea began to protest.

"Go!" He gave her a light shove. When she was out of sight he reached into the vase of silk flowers on the living room mantle and pulled two twenty dollar bills out of the roll of emergency money hidden at the bottom. He figured that should be enough for gas and some cheap tacos or something. Ralph tucked the bills in his pocket.

Half an hour later Ralph and Andrea stood on the lawn next to Ralph's bike. Andrea had changed into a soft green blouse with thin gold threads running through it. She'd paired it with her favorite blue jeans and her old, worn suede boots. She wore her hair pinned back from her face with shimmering gold combs. Ralph immediately noticed the blouse was a bit low cut, showing of soft, milky cleavage and that the jeans fit her hips in a way that was very complimentary.

"You look great," he said. "Did you get that at the mall today?"

Andrea snorted. "I didn't buy anything at the mall today. I bought this at Walmart last month."

Ralph gave her a skeptical look. "Six hours at the mall and you didn't buy a single thing?"

"I never do. The stuff's never that great, and it's way too expensive."

"Not a big spender, huh?"

"Never have been. I try not to buy anything I don't need."

"That's good, I guess."

"It's how dad raised us, always watching our pennies. Shelly's even worse than I am. She's never spent an unnecessary nickel in her life."

"Smart ladies," said Ralph. He handed her a helmet from the back of the bike. "You gotta have some fun once in awhile, though."

"We're taking the bike?" Andrea sounded a little panicked at the idea.

"Yep," said Ralph.

"We don't have to. I mean, I don't mind. We can take my car."

"We're taking the bike."

Andrea looked at it like it might bite her. "I've never been on one."

Ralph took the helmet from her hands and gently placed it on her head. He eased her arms into a spare leather jacket that matched the one he wore. "You'll love it."

Ralph straddled the bike. Andrea hesitated, then slid on behind him.

"Just hold tight, baby doll," Ralph said as he fired up the bike. "You're in for the ride of your life!"

They tore out of the driveway, engine thundering, as clumps of grass and mud flew up behind them. The noise of their departure echoed off the houses nearby.

Ralph sped up the twisting roads through the hills, leaving the town in the valley far below. They'd been riding for hours, going everywhere from City Park to the river and out to the fruit stand on the highway where Ralph had made a big deal out of buying Andrea a basket of fresh picked strawberries.

Now they stopped in the parking lot of the local golf course. The lights were off. No cars sat in the parking lot.

"Looks like they're closed," said Andrea.

"Not for us," said Ralph. He took a screwdriver from the bike's saddlebags. A moment later he popped the latch on the gate.

"Ralph!" Andrea cried in alarm.

"Not a problem. I know the owner." He swung the gate open. "Come on. I want to show you something."

He led Andrea through the gate and around a curve in the path. They walked a good distance before Ralph stopped between two trees. Andrea came up beside him.

"Wow," she said. They stood on the edge of a precipice. They could see the whole town spread out below. The lights glowed like little stars sprinkled across the valley. The air was so fresh and clear Andrea could see the traffic lights changing down on Main Street.

"It's amazing," Andrea continued. "I've never seen anything like it."

"Best view in town," said Ralph.

It took Andrea a moment to realize Ralph wasn't looking down at the town.

He was looking at her.

Long after Riley and the staff had gone home, William sat alone in the diner's office. A mix C.D. of his favorite Metallica songs played on the stereo behind him. "For Whom the Bell Tolls" filled his ears for the second time that day. An open bottle of scotch stood on the desk in front of him. He poured himself a glass and gulped it down. Finally ready, he eased open the very bottom drawer of the desk and reached his hand underneath it. He found the ziplock bag taped to the bottom and pulled it loose.

Oh so carefully, he slipped the blank sheet of paper out of the plastic and laid it on the desk. William studied it the way a great painter might study a canvas. It may have seemed like a mistake when he'd handed the sheet to Roger, but William had known exactly what he had been doing. This piece of paper was his insurance in case things ever got too serious with Roger. And now they had.

He poured himself another drink and sipped it slowly while he chose his next moves. At first he picked up a pen, then changed his mind and chose a bloody red marker instead. He made the first strokes tentatively, but soon got the flow going as he filled the page with large, red, angry letters.

When it was done he sat back, studying his handiwork and smoking a cigarette. "For Whom the Bell Tolls" had given way to "Ride the Lightening", which had been followed by "No Leaf Clover" and "Unforgiven". Now as William sat at the desk one last song came on.

"Don't tread on me," William said as he stubbed out his cigarette.

William remained blissfully unaware that across town, up in the hills, Andrea and Ralph still stood looking down at the lights below. The church bells began chiming out the hour. The sound washed over the valley in an ominous wave.

Chapter 6

Tell-Tale Ralph

In the morning, Ralph pulled Shelly aside when she came downstairs.

"I think you better move the money in the vase in the living room," he told her.

"What?" She asked. Her face showed total surprise. "Why?"

"I saw Mel in the living room yesterday. She took some money out of the vase and shoved it in her pocket."

Shelly hurried across the room. She took the vase down, pulled the money out and counted it. She stared at the bills in total disbelief and then counted them again. Still shaking her head, she counted them a third time.

"How bad is it?" asked Ralph.

"There's over a hundred dollars missing," said Shelly.

"Wow. She must be taking some every time she comes over or something."

"I have to tell Andrea."

Shelly headed for the kitchen. Ralph stopped her.

"Actually," he said, "maybe it's better if you don't."

"What?"

"You know how close they are," said Ralph. "It's really going to hurt Andrea if she finds out Mel's been taking the money."

"Yeah, you're right," Shelly said. She sounded dejected. "And Mel probably doesn't even realize what she's doing. She kinda lives in her own world, ya know?"

Ralph nodded sympathetically. "All the more reason to keep it our little secret."

"But what am I going to do, Ralph?"

"Give the money to me. I'll find a safe place for it."

Shelly handed over the wad of cash. "Thanks. You're a life saver."

"I'm just here to help."

William barged into the diner, looking frantic. He spotted Riley across the dining room and waved him over.

"Riley, Call the cops, Roger finally hit the big time."

"What happened?"

"He left this threatening note on my car."

Riley glanced at the note. His eyes widened and jaw dropped. Immediately, he called the cops. They arrived in twenty minutes. William got a bit nervous when they came to the diner due to all the memories of them coming for him years ago. The officer that showed up had no clue about William's past. Instead he knew that Moe's Diner donated money to the Fraternal Order of Police and New Laws program.

"You say you found this on your windshield?" Officer Bonney said.

"Yeah, I know it's from that Roger Delahoy kid."

The officer looked at it closely.

The note read, "*TAKE A LOOK TO THE SKY JUST BEFORE YOU DIE ITS THE LAST TIME YOU WILL.......*"

"Look at the psycho spiked letters. Every letter *I* is stabbed when it's dotted," Riley said.

"Whoever wrote this was very angry," the officer said as he put the note in a plastic sleeve and wrote up a report. William hoped they would take it seriously.

"We'll run it for prints and let you know," Bonney said. "Mr. Defreno, I may need some of your prints to eliminate them from the ones we find."

"Oh, you've got them on file already."

The officer left and Riley and William went back to working the lunch shift. They didn't have time to discuss what had just happened when a large table came in. They both waited the large table and were successful at making their experience at Moe's Diner one they would remember. After it was bussed they sat at the bar for a break.

"See, tax dollars at work. I hope they get that little loony bird off the streets. Anyone can see he's screwed up," Riley said.

"Yeah, yeah, I don't wanna discuss it," William insisted.

"Look, I know you didn't like calling the cops, but you had to. Who knows what that kid might do next."

"I said I know. Now can we drop it, please?"

Riley held his hands up in surrender. "Okay. It's dropped."

Ralph pulled into the driveway of an old battered farm house on the edge of town. He looked around let out a low whistle. He could not believe Andrea and Shelly's dad lived here. The place looked like a hurricane had hit a junkyard. Stuff was everywhere, including a beat up 1970s era pick up truck with a cracked windshield and flaking bright orange paint. Shelly had definitely been right; if she hadn't tipped him off he never would have guessed the guy had money. Ralph did a double take at an herb garden planted in an old cast iron bathtub. He wondered if the old man was a bit dodgy. In some ways that would be good, but it might also make things a bit more complicated. Folks kept a closer eye on relatives whose elevators didn't go all the way to the top.

He knocked on the front door. The guy who answered sure didn't look feeble mentally or physically. Hell, at 5'8" and a rock solid one hundred seventy pounds he looked like he might be in better shape than Ralph despite his old age. Come to that, he didn't even look old. Even though he was in his 60's life had not wrinkled his clean shaven face at all nor turned his crew cut hair gray. The only unpleasant part of his appearance was black teeth from chewing too much Red Man over the years. True he dressed in old work clothes so worn and stained they may as well have been rags, but you could never go by that.

"Hey there Austin," said Ralph. He offered his hand for a handshake. "Shelly called you about me helping you with your hot tub room."

"Hi. I haven't seen you since you were a little boy," the old man shook Ralph's hand with a grip that could crush rock. "Thanks for coming by."

"Yeah, you look the same."

"How's your mother doing?" Austin asked.

"Couldn't be better."

Austin stepped aside to let Ralph into the house. "Hot tub room's this way."

They turned down a hall to the left. Even from a distance Ralph could smell the mold and chlorine wafting out of the room at the end.

"Sorry the rest of the gang couldn't come by," said Ralph. "But you know how it is."

"Oh, I know. The kids have their lives. I'm sure Geoff's busy getting ready to leave tomorrow."

"Yeah. Man, is that guy a scatterbrain! I mean, no offense, but he's so disorganized I don't now how he ever gets anything done. So busy thinking about baseball he damn near walks into walls."

Austin chuckled. "That's my kid, alright. Took him to his first game when he was about five. He's been hooked ever since. I know this convention means the world to him. I don't begrudge him going. Kinda thought I might see the girls, though."

"They're at the mall."

"Again? I thought they went to the mall yesterday."

Whoops, thought Ralph. Definitely no flies on the old fella. He was sharp as a tack.

"They were," Ralph admitted. "Musta brought home a dozen bags full of crap. Then they turn around this morning and go back again. God knows what they'll buy next."

"I didn't realize they went shopping so often."

"Man, they practically live at that goddamn mall. I keep telling them not to buy so much stuff, but they just don't listen. No wonder all their credit cards are maxed out."

"What?" said Austin.

"Damn," Ralph looked sheepish. "Look, don't say anything. I don't think I'm supposed to know, but I heard them talking last night. They need a bunch of money fast or they may lose the house."

Austin suddenly stopped walking. He looked stricken.

"What?" asked Ralph.

"Shelly told me last night she wanted to talk about her inheritance," said Austin.

"Wow. They can't even wait 'til you're in the ground? I've seen some things in my time, but that's pretty damn cold."

"I'll talk to them. There has to be a way we can sort this out."

"Well, you could try," said Ralph. He sounded doubtful.

"But?"

"Ah, nothin'. Just forget it." Ralph started walking away. Austin stopped him.

"No, tell me. I need to know."

"I just got the impression they don't have much respect for you. Shelly said you were 'going goofy' and Andrea called you a 'crazy old coot'."

Austin looked heartbroken. "I had no idea," he said.

"Yeah. They seem to think you can't take care of yourself." Ralph hesitated, shook his head, and then continued. "They said something about getting your power of attorney."

"Really?" Austin slumped against the wall. For a second Ralph thought the old guy was having a heart attack, but after a few seconds he seemed alright.

"Man, I don't mean to tell you how to handle your business," said Ralph. "But if I were you I think I'd call me a lawyer."

Austin looked at him through tear glazed eyes. "Yeah. I think I'll do that."

William arrived at Andrea's house just as the sun was setting Tuesday evening. He found everyone gathered in the dining room. Andrea had prepared a mouthwatering meal of pork chops, baked apples and homemade macaroni and cheese- all of Geoff's favorites. William went to sit down then realized Ralph was in his usual spot. The only open chair was at the end of the table- next to Melissa. William sat down.

"Hey," Ralph said. He flashed William a gloating smile. "Glad you finally made it."

"You know how it is," said William. "Something always comes

up last minute."

"Yeah, tell me about it. When I was tiling the bathrooms at the World Trade Center something was always coming up. I'd start work at five in the morning and sometimes not get out of there 'til nine at night."

"Really, you did the tile?" An idea began to form in the back of William's brain. He was so sick of Ralph's made up B.S. Maybe he could finally call him out on it.

"Laid just about every single tile myself."

"I just redid a bunch of tile at the diner. Man, it was a pain in the ass."

"I bet doing all that tile at the World Trade Center was really tough," said Shelly.

"You have no idea," said Ralph.

"What do you like to use," asked William, "thin set mortar or that new alum based stuff?"

"Oh I've used 'em all, thin set, alum based. I don't have a preference. I'm they type of guy that can make work whatever he's given."

"You sure are," Shelly replied with a smile.

"Do you think the alum based mortar is worth the extra money?" William asked.

"I suppose, when we did the Trade Center the budget was pretty liberal."

"Oh, okay," William replied. He figured a guy who did all the tiles in the bathrooms at the World Trade Center would know there was no such thing as alum based mortar.

"Ya know," Melissa started. "America deserved to be bombed, all those people that died in New York deserved it."

"Why? They were just people going to work," William said.

"Cause they're New York losers. America sucks, and it was all staged anyway," she ranted in her earsplitting tone.

"So they deserved to die but aren't really dead?" William asked.

"God you're so stupid! Don't you know how these things work?"

"Do tell."

"They killed them all first and then staged the bombing."

"Jesus Christ! You're crazy!"

"William, stop!" said Andrea. "Can we please enjoy a meal in peace?"

"I'm game if the boys are." William looked toward the center of the table where Phillip and Thomas were flinging spoonfuls of macaroni and cheese at each other.

"They're children. You're not." Andrea's steely tone told William he'd better not push his luck.

"Duly noted." He said.

After dinner William helped Andrea clean up in the kitchen so they could have a little time alone.

"So honey, will you get me some alum based mortar next time you're at the Ace Hardware?" William said after he explained to Andrea there was no such thing.

"Oh, he probably didn't know if it was some new product or something. I don't think even the best construction managers keep track of all the building materials out there."

"Maybe not, but don't you think maybe he should know it's not possible to make an alum based mortar?"

Andrea shrugged. "Maybe it is."

William sighed in frustration.

"So, when does he plan to start this job building the Death Star all by himself?"

"Oh, stop. I don't know, it's not my business. He's been real helpful and he's not even gonna charge my dad. He may even help dad build an addition on his house."

"Won't that interfere with his work schedule?"

"He says he can work it out."

"Yeah, I bet."

"Hey," Andrea said. She nuzzled up close to him. "Wanna stay tonight?"

"I can't. I'll call you tomorrow."

William dropped the green and white dishtowel he was holding on the counter and walked out.

It was a long drive home. Even though the temperature on his new thermometer kept reading the same digits he could swear it got colder the farther he got from Andrea's house.

In the morning Ralph sat on the porch of Andrea's house, strumming his guitar and watching the hot blond across the street practice yoga in her sunroom. The Austin thing had caused him to reorder his priorities, but she was still very near the top of his "to-do" list. Just watching her made his jeans ache.

Andrea popped her head out of the front door.

"Hey," she said. "Dad just called. He said can you start Friday instead of Thursday? Something came up."

"Sure. No problem. I'll just stay here and write my next hit single." Ralph strummed his guitar. "What about you? Got any plans for today?"

"I was about to go feed Geoff's cat."

"Yeah?" Ralph stood up, making sure he kept his guitar in front him as he got to his feet. "I'll come with you."

Andrea unlocked the door to Geoff's apartment. Small but functional, the place was sparsely furnished. Baseball memorabilia covered every available inch of space. Geoff had organized it in a way that made it a stunning neat and orderly display instead of a wave of chaos. Heavy blackout curtains covered the living room windows, protecting the expensive collection from possible sun damage.

"Wow," said Ralph. "He could open his own museum."

"He just might one of these days."

Andrea crouched down at the end of the couch.

"Here, kitty, kitty," she called. "Hey, Ty, come out and say hello."

A beautiful smoke gray short haired cat slid out from under the couch. He stretched lazily before jumping up into Andrea's arms. Spotting Ralph, Ty narrowed his amber eyes and hissed.

"Now, Ty, be nice," said Andrea. The cat just growled in response. Andrea began scratching him behind the ears.

"Cute cat," Ralph said. He tried to make his gritted teeth look like a smile.

"Yeah, He's a sweetie. He doesn't meet many strangers, though."

Ralph spotted a small brown pile in the center of the rug.

"Ew, what's that?" he asked, though the smell made it obvious.

"Oh, he does that every time Geoff leaves town. It's his way of saying he's pissed about being left behind."

"Aw, man!"

"There should be some paper towels in the pantry."

Ralph went into the pantry. A half roll of paper towels sat on the lowest shelf. He knocked it into the trash with quick sweep of his arm and then closed the lid.

"No towels," he called to Andrea.

She came into the kitchen and took the cat's wet and dry food out of the cupboard over the sink.

"Try the bathroom," she said.

While Andrea finished mixing the dry and wet food, Ralph passed the hallway bathroom and went to the bathroom in Geoff's bedroom. He found a fresh roll of towels and brought them into the living room. Seeing that Andrea was still busy with the cat in the kitchen, Ralph ducked quickly back into the bedroom.

When he came back Andrea was cleaning up the mess on the rug.

"Hey, where did you disappear to?" she asked.

"Nowhere, baby doll. Been standing right here the whole time."

"Really?"

"Said your name and everything. You walked passed me like you didn't even hear me."

"Wow. I didn't even realize.... Sorry."

"I'll try not to be too hurt," Ralph said with a grin. "You okay, though? Where's your head at?"

Andrea shook her head. "Just lost in thought, I guess."

"Well there's nothing wrong with that. Just make sure you find your way back."

"To what?" Andrea asked.

Out behind the diner, William was taking advantage of the beautiful weather and a lull in diner business to wash both his cars. As he hand dried the water drops he noticed several scratches on the passenger side door of the Impala. Some of them looked deep enough to reach the car's undercoating.

His first thought was Roger, but the scratches were too low to the ground for a guy Roger's height to have made them. Then William remembered the boys playing near his car in the driveway the night before.

He knew he'd have to talk to Andrea and Shelly, but he didn't hold out much hope of it doing any good. The boys never seemed to face any consequences for anything.

Riley appeared at the back door of the diner. He held out the phone.

"It's the police."

"Oh," said William. Why didn't anyone ever call him on the diner's phone with good news? He took the phone.

"Hello," William said.

"Mr. Defreno? This is Detective Wilson. I just wanted to let you know we got a match back on the prints from that note on your car."

"You did?" William felt a little light headed. This was it.

"Yeah. Seems you were right. They match Roger Delahoy. Now, we've issued a warrant for his arrest, but he wasn't home when we went to pick him up. We expect to find him soon, but in the meantime you might want to be careful. Be extra vigilant. Lock your doors and windows and try to make sure you stay around other people."

"Thanks," said William. "I'll do that."

He hung up the phone.

"They got him?" Riley asked.

"Not yet, but they will."

"That's a good thing, William. That kid's a menace."

"Yeah, yeah. It's a good thing."

The rest of the day and evening passed in a blur. William didn't go to Andrea's. Instead he stayed at the bar through closing, and long after. Once again he found himself having a few too many and then falling into his bed at dawn.

Ralph spent most of the next day working on the hot tub room with Austin. The old man had demo'ed the old tile walls himself over the preceding days. Probably working out his anger, Ralph figured. Thankfully stuff had been in pretty good shape behind the tile and the work moved quickly. With the pace they were going they could be finished in three days or less. They spent the morning hanging the last pieces of new cement board to prepare for tiling. Austin was getting more cement backboard ready for Ralph to attach to the beams when he stepped on the pencil they were using to trace the beams on the board with the T square.

"Go get another pencil off my desk in the office," Austin said to Ralph.

"Okay, I'm gonna use the pisser too."

Ralph went to the office and grabbed a pencil from the cup full of writing utensils. A stack of legal looking papers sat in the center of the desk. Ralph skipped his trip to the bathroom to look them over. After scanning them quickly, he went back to Austin.

"Whew, that's lookin' good," Ralph said, nodding at the half built wall.

"Yeah, but it's rough puttin' this stuff up with just two of us."

"Well, I wouldn't count on getting any help."

Austin's face fell. "Yeah, I know."

"So what happened yesterday?"

"I took your advice." Austin sat down on an upturned bucket and mopped his face with a handy rag. "Had a meeting with my lawyer."

"Oh." Ralph pretended to look surprised. "What did he say?"

"First, he recommended I replace my will with a living trust. I set myself up as both trustor and trustee and then name a back up trustor and the kids as secondary trustees. There are no estate taxes and no probate court to deal with. The transfer happens automatically upon my death."

"Really?"

"Yeah. Great thing, that. I was afraid half of what I had or more was gonna end up going to the government. And I can still leave some of my wealth to charity. The church is getting ten percent, and I plan to leave something to that New Laws program everyone's talking about. They do some good work."

"I've heard of them, they go around and scare the kids into behaving themselves. I'd be real good at that job, I'd love to do that all day."

Austin laughed. "The other thing my attorney recommended is that I complete a power of attorney now, so that if I'm ever declared unable to handle my own affairs someone of my own choosing takes charge."

"Did you have someone in mind?"

"Well, I was thinking about Geoff, but like you said, he's kind of scatterbrained."

"Yeah. He is. And he doesn't always have the best sense. He'd probably blow ten thousand bucks for toilet paper used by Babe Ruth or something." Ralph thought for a minute. "What you need is a neutral party, someone who will be fair to everyone and look out for you, too. Someone who has no vested interest in what happens to you or your money."

"Yeah, that's a good idea, but I don't know anybody like that."

"Well what about someone from church?"

"I don't know any of them that well. And none of them know the kids at all. I don't think they'd like having a stranger in charge."

"Maybe that's what they need, though. Someone stern who can play daddy and rein them in when you're gone."

"Maybe." Austin shook his head. "I tell you, it's a tough decision. I mean if you can't trust your family, who can you trust?"

"Don't worry, Austin," Ralph said solicitously. "I'm sure you're think of someone."

Friday night William arrived at Andrea's late after the dinner shift was done. The place was not nearly as clean as it should have been with Ralph there supposedly earning his keep through work. When he walked in the kitchen, he could hear Ralph telling some outlandish story to all of them. William listened in before letting everyone know he was there.

"And there I was," Ralph said. "These guys had disabled my car by cutting the battery cable. There was like fifteen of 'em with baseball bats. I had nothing, I mean nothing but my bare fists. I walked up to their leader and told 'em this was an unfair fight. There's only fifteen of you guys with weapons verses one of me in my bare hands, that's not fair to you guys."

"Wow, what did they say?" Shelly wondered.

"They dropped the bats and took off. I told 'em I'd be sending them a bill for the new battery cable."

"Weren't you scared?" Shelly said.

"A little, but I knew they were nothing compared to me."

"Hello," William said.

"Hey, hun," Andrea said.

William could see that he'd missed dinner. That was fine by him. He loved Andrea, but didn't think he could stomach eating another meal while listening to Ralph spouting manure.

Andrea had a fresh peach cobbler in the kitchen, though. Shelly took the boys upstairs to wash up while Andrea went into the kitchen to serve up dessert. William and Ralph went into the dining room. Soon everyone was settled around the table and Andrea passed out bowls of warm cobbler topped with vanilla ice cream.

"How's the working on the hot tub room coming?" Andrea asked Ralph.

"Oh man, that room is a mess! We got the wall open today and everything behind it's rotten. Looks like a pipe's been leaking. We're going to have to put in new framing, new plumbing, new wiring, everything. We're gonna be working on that room for weeks."

"Wow, I didn't realize it was that bad," said Shelley.

"Man, that whole place is a wreck. Have you seen how much stuff your dad has?"

"Yeah I know," Andrea said. "It would be hard to go through it all if he died. I don't wanna just throw it all away in case some of it's valuable. I don't know how to divide it all. I wanna make sure everything gets sold for it's full value and not waste any of it."

"Dividing that stuff is a big job, I wonder whose gonna get that fun job?" Ralph said.

"I don't know." Andrea said. "All of us will be good-hearted about it, none of us are interested in ripping off the others."

"Things change when money's involved."

"Naa, it won't. I'm gonna just put my share in some safe CD's or bonds or something."

"Not gonna go out and by yourself your own custom Harley?"

Andrea turned pink. "Yeah, right."

"How about a shiny new car?"

"I don't think so. The one I have is only about six years old, and a good car lasts a long time. I don't think I'll need another one for a long time."

"It can take quite a lot of skills to be fair. Lots of people don't have the morals to be fair. But I'm glad you guys are like I am."

"Yes, me too."

"I know if I were in charge of distributing everything, I'd be fair," Ralph said. For no more than a moment Ralph's eyes rolled to the side and a sinister smirk came to his face. It was so fast nobody but William noticed. The split second gaze reminded William of something a serial killer like Charles Manson or Ted Bundy would do. It was like some ominous thought of Ralph's overflowed into his face without the man even realizing it. William didn't know if it was a slip up or if Ralph was so foul he just couldn't help expressing it.

William was sure that Ralph didn't intentionally make any expression and was planning some sort of way to steal their inheritance. It reminded him of the character in "The Tell-Tale Heart" that talked with the detectives the exact spot where the old man was buried under the floorboards. William wondered if like the character in the old novel, Ralph mentioned their dad's inheritance and that he would be fair just for the same perverted ecstasy emotions the character in the book got.

After dessert William helped Andrea put the plates in the dishwasher. He wanted to ask her what the deal with Ralph was, but every time he tried to bring it up she changed the subject.

After a few minutes Shelly and Ralph joined them in the kitchen. The boys ran past them, chasing each other and screaming about something. They knocked over a T.V. tray without even noticing it. Even worse was when Thomas picked up the T.V. tray and without a thought of consequence, threw it at Phillip. It crashed to the ground and broke into pieces. Shelly picked up the pieces and threw them away without a word to them about what just happened. The boys continued to run wildly through the house, screaming and throwing things.

William shook his head. "Little O.J. one and two," he said.

"O.J. one and two?" Shelly said.

"Yeah, that's what I call the boys, cause like O.J. Simpson they get away with murder."

Andrea rolled her eyes. "They're just kids, William."

"I know, but they do a lot of damage. They scratched my car yesterday."

"Sorry, William, that's what's gonna happens with kids. You can buff it out, right?"

"Yeah, I can, but that's not the point. They need to stay away from people's cars. They could get hurt."

"Come here boys," Andrea said.

"Whaaaat," Thomas replied.

"You guys scratched William's car with your bikes. That's not nice. You guys stay away from his car," Andrea said to the boys who just stared in silence.

"Yeah," Shelly added. "Stay away from peoples cars."

"Blaaaa," Thomas responded as he stuck his tongue out and giggled. Both of them ran off trying to tag each other. Nobody seemed to care and they rough-housed some more. They chased each other through the house screaming as loud as they could. In William's opinion they didn't get nearly enough retribution for scratching his car. He wondered if they even took note to the fact that they were told not to do it again.

"There, happy?" Shelly asked.

"I guess so. I'm not convinced they're gonna stay away from it, though. I guess when they grow up I'll have a shop fix the scratches. No point in doing it now, they're just gonna do it again."

"I know they're a handful sometimes, They scratch my car too." Shelly said.

A loud series of crashes came from the other room where the boys were playing. The last crash had a deep musical tone to it. They all went to living room to see what happened. The loud musical tone was from Ralph's guitar falling over because of their fooling around. Shelly's eyes got large and she darted toward the guitar.

"Oh my god, is the guitar okay?" She asked as she handed it to Ralph.

"It's fine, it falls over all the time," he replied.

"You little assholes!" Shelly screamed at the boys. "Get over here." They didn't come so she grabbed them and gave each of them seven to eight swats on their behinds as hard as she could. They started to cry and Shelly didn't care and swatted them more. This came as a huge surprise to William since they usually could do whatever they wanted without punishment. Their crying had very little effect of Shelly.

"You could've broken his guitar! Both of you are grounded! Go to your rooms, now! Get the hell outta here!" She screamed. This time they listened as they moved slowly toward their rooms..

"Mommy," sniffle sniffle. "What does grounded mean?" Thomas asked.

"It means no T.V., no Xbox, no Playstation, no Nintendo Wii, no internet, no Facebook, no cell phone, 'til I say so!"

"What about my Ipad?" Phillip wondered.

"No!"

"What are we suppose to do all day?" Thomas whined and began to cry again.

"Hey," Shelly continued. "You're not movin' fast enough! I said get the hell outta here!" Both of them speed up and went to their rooms sobbing.

William laughed to himself that with the exception of T.V. none of the stuff she mentioned existed throughout his entire childhood. Instead of Facebook friends he remembered having real friends. Memories of playing dodgeball, baseball, Chutes and Ladders, cowboys and Indians, riding bikes and going to Circle K came to mind. They would all make up games to play if there was nothing else. It might have been pretending their bikes were race cars or pretending to go on journeys to other planets.

One in particular came to mind. Him, Mitch and Riley would often play a wintertime game in Riley's parents' pitch dark backyard called "War in Vietnam". Nobody could see anything it was so dark and they would throw snowballs at each other and hope they hit someone. The memory of getting an icy snowball right in face without warning made him laugh. Although, he knew even though he made it fine without all that tech garbage, the boys would suffer immensely without it

"Are you sure the guitar's okay? If there is damage I'll pay for it," Shelly said to Ralph.

"It's fine."

After the chaos died down a cheerless William got to have some time with Andrea. Usually, no matter what they talked about it was always fun and relaxing. Tonight, he hardly enjoyed his drink and cigarettes. She looked away as he tried to talk to her about funny customers at the diner. William knew if Ralph wanted to talk to her she would be attentive and excited. He felt his good days with her were in its closing stages and were drifting apart. At first he was saddened by Ralph making her so distant from him. In the last few days he felt comfort in that distance.

He decided to give up on telling funny stories from work and instead dive right into the Ralph situation.

"How's it going with Ralph's new job?" he asked.

"They keep delaying him."

"Who's he supposed to be working for, anyway? What's the company?"

"I don't know. I think he said it was Acme Contracting or something."

"What? 'Meep, meep?'" William said with sarcasm. "Come on, are they really going to start building high rise buildings in this town? And did you see the look on his face when he said he'd be fair about dividing your dad' s stuff? What the hell was that all about? "

"Oh stop! What look? Why does it bother you so much? You been like jealous of him from day one."

"Well you guys treat him like the pharaoh and I'm telling you he's up to something. That look, I don't think he even knew he made it."

"William honey, you don't need to shoot him down. He is who he is and you are who you are. I love you for who you are You don't have to be someone like Ralph."

William left her house after a little while. For the first time he was happy to leave her house and go to the diner to drink at the bar. He pondered what that comment meant. It was certain that she basically was saying "Ralph is the great in every way, but don't worry. I love you even though you're a huge loser compared to him."

As rough as that was, at least he knew where he stood.

Chapter 7

Kiss It Goodbye

William and Riley stood at the bar in the diner. They stared out the big picture windows at the traffic zipping by. The lunch had been uncharacteristically slow so far. For the first time since they'd opened, less than half the tables were full.

"I knew it," said William. "I knew that hacked website was going to screw us over."

"It'll pass," said Riley. "Our real website's up again, we've mailed out fliers offering a free appetizer and that article about your donation to the no-kill shelter is running in tomorrow's paper. We'll have this place full again in no time."

"Good work, Riley. You are a genius when it comes to P.R."

"Thanks. You can't turn a blind eye to these things, you know."

"Speaking of blind eyes, I'm glad people in this town got their eye surgeries," William replied in a loud and happy tone.

"What?"

"Did you know people in this town used to be blind with cataracts? When the Casners were dictators they would not allow any eye surgeons to come in the town to cure people."

"Oh my sweet lord," Riley said and put his hands over his face.

"Yep, but one was smart and said that if he could come in and cure the people they would no longer be blind and they would be able to see the Casners better. Even the blind people went on and on that they were so depressed that they never saw Randy or Carol."

"Really?"

"Yep. So the doctor did the surgeries, but halfway through almost got kicked out of the city."

"Gee, why was that?" Riley said sarcastically.

"The doctor wanted to get a picture of the bronze statue of Randy. It was so big that he had to lay down to get it all in view. When the cops saw that they told him that 'you never lie down in front of the statue of Randy.' The cops even said they were scared of what could happen to them for allowing the doctor to lay down in front of it for as long as he did. It almost got the doctor kicked out of town and all the blind people would've been screwed."

"Well, I'm glad they had compassion."

"Well, it was only because Randy and Carol wanted those people to be able to see them better. Even after the doctor was done, the people had to give their thanks to Randy and Carol. Not even one kind word was said to the doctor."

"Well buddy, I'm so glad you defeated those Casners. Sounds like complete hell around here with them around."

The boredom dragged on. Usually when it was this slow he'd just take off and go visit Andrea and her family. He didn't feel like doing that today, though. William could imagine the girls fawning over Ralph, listening to his tough guy stories and crazy boasts with astonishment. He didn't think he could stomach it. He wished something exciting would happen.

It didn't take long for that wish to come true.

The sounds of police sirens coming from outside became louder and louder. Both William and Riley heard the sound of tires screeching and police officers screaming commands. The noise was coming from right outside the diner. A young man barged through the front door, out of breath with his clothes shredded. From behind, several cops grabbed him and threw him to the ground.

"Get the fuck off me! Ahhhhh, get the fuck off me!" The young man bellowed. The kid was slippery enough to slip right through the cops' grip and stand back up. Normally it would upset William to see a kid barge through the door and fight with the cops while screaming obscenities but one look at the young man was all it took to identify him as Roger Delahoy.

"So what did you do this time?" William asked Roger, who came up the bar to see Riley and William.

"You know what I did, but I didn't do it! You know I didn't do

94

it!"

The cops caught up to Roger and slammed him to the ground. They all wrestled for a while and more swearing and screaming came from Roger. William knew this was probably about the threatening note on the car. Although he was hoping they would break Rogers chops, he wasn't expecting such a showdown and direct confrontation.

"I didn't write that note, William. You know I didn't. I don't know how my prints got on it, but I didn't do it," Roger bellowed as the cops used their force to subdue him.

"Quit resisting, now!" The cops demanded.

"I am not resisting arrest! Get the fuck off me, you cocksuckers! I am not resisting arrest!" Roger cried out as he violently resisted arrest.

William could only chuckle at Roger's statement. How could he not think he was resisting? The screaming and breaking away from them along with fighting seemed like textbook resistance. If what Roger was doing was not resisting arrest, it would be mind boggling to think what would be. It seemed Roger was only going to get himself deeper in trouble.

"You know I didn't do this William. You know I didn't!"

"Didn't do what?" William asked.

"The threatin' letter man, I didn't write it."

Police got the cuffs on him. William's heartbeat jumped as he realized Roger was telling the truth. The letter was just revenge for the website break in that Roger really did do. The screaming continued until the cops got Roger to stand up. Finally he calmed down. One of the officers approached William.

"Want to press trespassing charges to for him breaking in here like this?"

"Nah, seems like he's already in trouble."

The cops were fairly composed and professional considering what had just happened. It seemed like this would be an easy arrest that would end quietly. That all changed abruptly when an officer searched Roger's pockets and found an eighth of an ounce of marijuana. The officer gasped in rage and his eyes got wide as he breathed heavily.

"What's this?" The officer said in a lax tone that was building fast to fury. "What...is... thiiiis? What is it?" He screeched out. "What is it, huh?" he barked, six inches from Roger's face. "Get on the God damn ground, noooow!"

"William," Roger cried out. "Help me, please."

"Please get him outta here," William replied.

The cops bagged the drug evidence and began to read Roger his rights. Roger just nodded his head and once the adrenalin wore off the reality that he was in immense trouble with the law set in. He hung his head in shame. As they started to haul him away Roger cried out some more to William.

"I guess I'll see you in court, Mr. Casner," Roger said.

"What? Hold on officers," William said. The officer paused the process of hauling Roger away. "What did you call me, boy?"

"I might have been four years old when the shit went down, but I remember you. Being expelled, the arrest, the meth lab the Casners had. Fourteen years, remember? I know everything, William."

"Why you callin' me Mr. Casner?"

"Cause, you became him, didn't you? Own a business, bribed the school to take away my track record, donating to programs like New Laws and crap. And now you framed me, just like he framed you. Just like him, you're obsessed with some glory days from high school."

"Whatever, kid. You need help."

"I bet that's what they said about you! You framed me, William, you know it."

"Get him outta here," William stated.

The cops took Roger to the police car while William spoke with the remaining cops. William felt about ready to faint. His face was pale and legs were like gelatin after the statements Roger made. Still, he kept his composure as he spoke to the officers in a professional manner. Nobody seemed to notice he was being eating up inside. They took a witness statement and were ready to rap things up.

"You can relax now. He won't be bothering you anymore," The officer said.

"Yeah, I mean I just really want him to not write me that crap anymore ya know?"

"Well we will keep you posted on court dates and the outcome of his arrest today."

"Yeah, please do."

The officers left and William and Riley went back to the lunch shift. William put on quite an act for Riley about Roger's statement. His hands were shaking, though. Not once, but twice, drinks he was serving slipped right through his hands and crashed on the floor.

"Hey man, you okay?" asked Riley.

"Yeah," William mopped his forehead with a towel from the bar. "It's all those cops and the sirens and all. You'd think I'd be immune to it by now, but even when I know they aren't coming for me, they scare me shitless every time."

"I've actually heard that's pretty common for those who've had run-ins with the law," said Riley. He smiled mischievously. "I believe they call it five-o-phobia."

"Nice to know it has a name. Listen, I think I need to get out of here for awhile. Get some fresh air, you know?"

Riley nodded. William grabbed his keys and darted out the back door of the diner like the devil was chasing him.

Behind the wheel of the Impala, William felt a little calmer. He took a few deep breaths and pulled out of the parking lot. After driving several miles along the highway, he suddenly realized he didn't have a destination in mind. When he thought about it, though, William realized he only had one place to go. Before long he found himself pulling into Andrea's driveway.

Ralph's bike sat by the back door. It was surrounded by tools, puddles of grease and empty boxes that, according to their labels, had held high performance parts. William sighed with relief. Maybe Ralph had finally started working and this whole ordeal would be over soon.

When he entered the house he wondered if he had the right house because there was too much peace and silence. Then he saw the two boys quietly enjoying a coloring book in the living room.

"Gee, they can behave," William said to himself as he entered the dining room where Ralph was eating a nice T-bone steak with salad.

"Can I get you more salad Ralph?" Shelly asked.

"Naa,"

"Bread and butter maybe?"

"Naa, gotta get to yer dads and do more tile."

"Try my cherry pie, it's really good."

"Well, I got time for a slice."

William laughed. "Tastes so good, makes a grown man cry," he sang to himself. Nobody else heard him, though and he didn't feel like repeating it. Feeling ignored, he walked into the living room, but stayed where he could see the group in the dining room.

"Oh man, that's good," Ralph said as he finished the pie. He pushed the plate away and patted his stomach. "Anybody seen my work shirt?"

"It should be in the laundry basket on the couch," Shelly said. "I washed all your clothes for you this morning."

"Cool, that motorcycle exhaust makes 'em stink."

"You ever gonna get a real motorcycle?" An annoying female voice said. William cringed to see that Melissa was there again to mooch up some free food and annoy anyone she could. He wondered if anything positive every came from her mouth. She sat and stared at William with a look that said just his existence pissed her off. Ralph ignored the comment and continued to get ready to leave.

Ralph came into the living room. William saw him pull a pharmacy bag out of Shelly's purse to see what was inside. He shook the bottles for fun and looked at the labels. The bottles of pills were ADHD medicine for the boys. Ralph laughed and handed the pill bottles to William.

"Oh wow," William said as he looked at the bottles of Ritalin and Tenex.

"What the hell are you doing snooping through my stuff William?" Shelly barked as she came in the room. Andrea heard and joined in as well.

"William," Andrea snapped. "Quit poking around in their meds. It's none of your damn business what pills we're giving the boys."

William froze like a deer in the headlights for a moment. Memories of the police and his old friends Frank and Joe tag-teaming him flashbacked in his mind. Even if he had been snooping it seemed they were overreacting. He didn't know whether to hand the pills back or start defending himself. Both of the girls continued to huff and puff about his alleged snooping. Before he could respond Ralph intervened.

"Whoa," Ralph said. "Just calm down girls. William's been falsely accused. I'm the one who grabbed it out of your purse. I was just showing it to him."

"Oh," Shelly said. Immediately the girls dropped their ruthless tones.

"Well," Shelly said in a gentle voice. "Please just ask, I would've shown you. I don't like putting the kids on meds, but I felt I have no choice."

"Yeah," Andrea added in a delicate voice. "Maybe you can give us advice on if you think the pills are good. You had said you were a doctor at one time in the Army."

"Well, today's meds are over-prescribed in my opinion, but I do think the boys could benefit from such things as right-a-lin"

"You mean *Rit*-a-lin," William said.

"Yeah, yeah that's right. I just pronounce it differently. Cause, ya know, that's they way they pronounce it in Belgium where I got my medical training." Ralph stated.

"Wow, you've been everywhere," said Shelly.

"Just about." Ralph looked at the clock. "Oh man! I was gonna wax the bike before going over to Austin's. Looks like I'm out of time, though."

"I'll wax it," said Shelly. "Just take Andrea's car for now."

"Are you sure? I mean it's gotta have two coats of Turtle Wax or the summer sun is gonna trash the paint. It'll be a lot of work."

"I don't mind. If I get tired I'll make Andrea come help."

"You're a peach." Ralph leaned over and kissed Shelly on the cheek. "I'm out of here. Bye everybody." He waved to Andrea and Shelly. Instead of a wave for Melissa, she got the middle finger as he left.

William smirked. Melissa glared at him and then flipped him off the way Ralph had done to her.

"Aw, how cute, you can count to one," said William.

"Don't talk to my friend like that," said Andrea. She stalked back into the kitchen.

"She started it!" William protested as he followed her into the kitchen.

"That doesn't mean you have to respond. Can't you please act like an adult for a change? What are you even doing here? Aren't you supposed to be working?"

Since when did he need a reason to stop by? Immediately his idea of talking to Andrea about the morning's ordeal and Roger comparing him to Randy Casner left his mind. He came up with a quick lie instead.

"I was just in the neighborhood," he said. "Thought I'd come say hi and see if you needed anything at the store."

"Nope. We're all doing just fine without you." She dropped a lid onto a pot with a loud clang. William noticed the red sauce that splashed out from around the lid's edges.

"Spaghetti, huh?" William said. He was disappointed. It wasn't that he didn't like spaghetti, he just wondered why Ralph got better food served to him like a sultan.

"Ya know, I gotta start cuttin' back on things. I gotta be able to get a boiler when winter comes," Andrea said.

"I thought Ralph was gonna buy you a new furnace with the money from this new job."

"He still hasn't started yet, and even when he does I don't want to put that burden on him. He's been working hard for my dad. I don't think he should have to buy me a furnace on top of it."

"Oh," said William.

"You're the one who owns a diner, maybe you should eat there once in while."

"I thought you liked having me come over for dinner."

"I do. I just wish you'd bring something or help out every once in awhile."

Someone started banging loudly on the front door. William went to answer so he didn't have to respond to Andrea. Geoff stood at the door, looking wild eyed and frantic.

"Hey, when did you get back?" William asked.

"Couple hours ago. Where's Andrea?"

"In the kitchen. Hang on." William turned to call for her, but Geoff pushed past him. Hearing her brother's voice, Andrea came into the living room.

"Hey Geoff, what's up?"

Loud psychotic swearing and screams of sorrow started as soon as Geoff saw her. It seemed to William the day had already been exciting enough and whatever this was didn't need to happen. The swearing and screaming got louder while they all stood and stared.

"Geoff, what's the matter?" Andrea asked.

"It's gone Andrea! My Roger Maris card is gone!"

"How can that be?"

"I don't know!" Geoff yelled.

"Here have some water and settle down," Andrea said as he got Geoff a drink. Geoff took his glass and made a trip to the bathroom. The door slammed and wobbled the house. William passed by the bathroom and heard Geoff's icy breath whisper screams of pain. Everyone knew how much that baseball card meant to him and that there would be no sleep till it was found.

"Did you leave the door unlocked or something when you fed his cat?" William asked Andrea.

"No, we made sure it was all secure. Maybe he just misplaced it."

"We? Who's we?"

"Me and Ralph went over there."

"Why did he go?"

"Just to help. He's been very helpful around here."

"It takes two people to feed a cat?"

"He just really wanted to help."

"Did he take it?"

"Oh, that's impossible, Geoff just lost it that's all."

"Where did Ralph get money for high performance parts for the bike?"

"I don't know, William. It's not really my business."

Geoff finally came out of the bathroom. Andrea guided him into the living room and sat him down on the couch. He hugged himself as he rocked back and forth on the center cushion. Shelly took his hand and began reassuring him that the card was probably just misplaced. He nodded, seeming desperate to believe that was true and that it would soon turn up.

"Just go buy a new one," said Melissa. "I don't know what you're so upset for. Baseball's stupid anyway."

"You can't just buy a new Roger Maris card," said William. "They don't make them anymore."

Geoff moaned and clutched his head. "It's gone, it's gone, it's gone."

"You know, William, this is really a family matter," said Andrea. "Maybe you should go."

William looked at Melissa, who obviously wasn't being asked to leave, and then back at Andrea.

"Yeah, maybe I should."

With no place else to go, William drove back to the diner. Business had picked up. The place was packed. Despite it being busy, William didn't dive into work. Instead he sat down at the bar and poured himself a drink. Riley came over to see what was up.

"Feeling better?" he asked.

"Not really." William told him about events at Andrea's: the missing card, the girls doting on Ralph, how he got steak while everyone else got spaghetti, Andrea saying William never helped out even though he was the only one who gave her a hand or brought things for meals and how Melissa had been allowed to stay despite her rude comments even though William had been asked to leave.

"Wow," said Riley.

"I really don't know what to do about this Ralph thing and Andrea."

"I know. You've been mentioning concerns since the day he got there, but I didn't think it was this bad."

"He's like a God to them. I feel like when I go over I imagine the boys are fanning him with big feathers, Andrea's peeling him a grape and Shelly's shining his shoes. I mean he's just untouchable. He can do no wrong."

"I guess they really like him."

"They worship him. Like today, they were yelling at me cause they thought I was snooping through the boy's medications. When they found out it was Ralph they were like; 'oh Ralph did it, well then it's allllll-riiiight now, in fact it's a gas," William said and tried to sing lyrics from The Rolling Stones "Jumpin' Jack Flash".

"I'm sorry to hear that."

"That Melissa is the same way. She can do no wrong. I feel like asking Andrea how I can get on the untouchables list these guys are on. I mean they're gonna be out there waxing his bike all day even though he's living there for free. Shouldn't he be waxing her car?"

"William, you know I'm always the bearer of bad news, but this guy just brings something to the table that you don't. That's the bottom line."

"But what? Everything he says is a lie. I don't even think he ever had a job coming to him. He's obnoxious. I think he's ugly, too. You know what? He's not even a good con artist. I mean why is he flat broke if he's so cunning? Why doesn't he have some island with ten wives and goons and monkey butlers or something? It's been killing me! What does he give them?"

"It's not always something that can be explained. He just warmed them up. They may just be infatuated by him. Sometimes a person just likes something about the other person. For example, did you see a few years ago Hulk Hogan's wife Linda Hogan left him? She had to split up everything she had, the big house, the sports cars. She lost half her net worth. I mean she gave up being with the big, strong, famous, rich Hulk Hogan and ran off with some scrawny twenty-year-old working at Taco Bell. Why? He just gave her something Hulk couldn't. What it is ain't exactly clear."

"Well, maybe Linda left him because the twenty-year-old was cute or she could dominate him or something. I mean she didn't leave him for some bull-shittin' con artist."

"Ya know, William, the girls might not believe everything he says. Maybe they don't care. They might know everything he says is crap, but they excuse it for some reason. It can't be explained. No science in the world can explain human love. He's got something you don't. He just sparks their soul or something."

"He sure does."

"Look, some guys just know how to play ball. They know what women want. Haven't you seen these like ugly, stupid, jerky guys with like Bar Refaeli lookin' girls? They knew what to do and they were blessed with that spark."

"So you're saying God just likes those guys better?"

"I don't know if I'd go that far, but God blesses everyone differently."

"Except me. I don't need an alarm clock. I wake up every morning at the same time to God spitting in my face."

"William, don't be talkin' smack about the man upstairs." Riley said and crossed his arms while he glared at William.

"I'm sorry, Riley. I went too far. I guess I must not have that spark. Plus years of fighting wars probably killed my spark and ate my soul. I need soul retrieval."

"What?"

"Oh, this customer that came in last week does soul retrieval. She explained all about it that trauma or loss can make pieces of the soul go away and leave you feeling dead."

"Maybe it's more than just some spiritual thing. It could even be that you never had a dad. That can dampen your spark or whatever by not having that male role model in your life."

"It's something like that. Having a loving relationship is just not in my cards."

"Or it's a bigger challenge. This Ralph guy may be good with relationships, but might be bad at other things."

"I don't know if he's even the lover boy we think he is. Could he do it again? If he got thrown out could he just find another set of girls who would let him live for free and treat him like he's Ramesses?"

"Maybe, maybe not. Sometimes God gives you a break, but only one, not two."

"So what can I do? If I demand he leaves or I leave, I'm not even sure that I'll be chosen. Even if they do choose me then I'm always gonna be the bad guy that chased away their savior."

"Maybe he'll leave on his own and be forgotten about. If you push for him to leave you'll probably win, but like you said, he'll always be a saint. Let him crash and burn and if they don't figure it out, then you're better off without them."

"That's easy to say in theory, but I really wasn't planning on trying to date again in life. It's pissing me off that this guy came in and just swept them off their feet. Besides, working at her dad's house is shit. He's up to something. I'm not crazy when I said he had this like secret smile and like rolled his eyes when he was saying he would divide everything fairly."

"Yeah, I know you don't wanna break up, but maybe you need to find someone who *celebrates* you not *tolerates* you."

"That's brilliant, Riley. That's exactly what's happening. I'm being tolerated and he's being celebrated."

"Give him enough rope to hang himself. He will. You can't build a house on bullshit."

"Yeah, hopefully," William replied and shook his head.

"Well, I better get back to work. You gonna join me or just sit there and drink all night?"

"Think I'll stay here. I'm gonna be in the alcohol of fame any day now."

Ralph and Austin sat in the gazebo out behind Austin's place drinking a twelve pack and watching the sun go down. They'd gotten more good work done on the hot tub room and were rewarding themselves with a break. Mostly they talked about nothing, but as it grew later and the beer case got emptier Austin's tongue loosened. Ralph carefully waited for the right moment before bringing up what he really wanted to talk about.

"So how's trust paperwork coming?" he asked as Austin crushed his third empty beer can and dropped it in the grass.

"Oh, you know lawyers," said Austin. He cracked open another can of beer. It hissed loudly in the quiet night. "The longer it takes the more they get paid."

"Yeah, I know," said Ralph.

"Gotta finish it soon, though. I think my time might be running out."

"Oh man, did you get bad news?" Ralph looked genuinely surprised. He hoped surprise was the right reaction. Surprise, or concern? Both maybe? Man, figuring out the right reactions to stuff was hard sometimes.

Austin shook is head. "Don't worry, I'm fine."

Ralph breathed a sigh of relief. He'd gotten the reaction right. "What's goin' on then?" he asked Austin.

"Shelly asked me for ten-thousand dollars. She claims it's for some cockamamie school for something. Dental hygiene or something like that."

"Well that would be good, wouldn't it? I mean if she went to school she could make more money."

"Maybe, but I know Shelly. If she went to school she'd been

studying to be a teacher or something. I can't see her as a dentist. She doesn't like science and she hates germs."

"So you don't think she really wanted the money for school?"

"Well, like I said, it's out of character. I might have bought it, though, if I hadn't had that heads up from you. Thanks again for that, by the way."

Ralph shook his head. "Well, you're welcome. I'm just sorry I turned out to be right. Man, it pisses me off to see the way they treat you."

"It's alright."

"No, man, it isn't! It ain't alright at all! It pisses me off! They just don't appreciate you at all. I mean I never had a dad and here they've got a great one and they treat you like you're some piggy bank they can't wait to break open."

"Really? I never knew you grew up with just your mom."

"I did though, man, I did." Ralph chugged his beer. "Man of the house since the time I could fuckin' walk, man, that's what I was. Took care of me, took care of the house, took care of my brother and sister. Even took care of mom. There I was, nine years old and balancing her checkbook. Man, that woman could spend money. I made sure the bills got paid, told her how much we had left and how much she could spend. I basically had to give her an allowance."

"Man, that's rough," said Austin.

"Oh it was, man, it was. You should have seen me. I had to stand on a chair to reach the counter to pay the water bill. And the grocery store, cause you know if I didn't shop we didn't eat, I was so short I couldn't even reach to give the cashier the money. She had to come around and get it from me. I remember this one time, man, I was counting out pennies to buy milk for the kids. She just looked at me with these big sad eyes."

"You know, I knew your mom. She was a teller at my bank way back when. Pretty lady."

"That she was. It made me proud to keep her together. Looking at her no one would have guessed what was going on at home. The booze, the men... but I knew she'd get fired if they found out, so I held it together. I made sure she was at work on time, clear headed and clean every single day no matter what it cost me."

"Must have made you quite the tough little fella."

"It did, man, it did. I'm glad for it though." Ralph thumped himself on his chest. "Made me who I am."

"Good for you," said Austin. He toasted Ralph with his beer can.

"Man, I remember this one year... I'd been saving all summer for a fishing pole. Geoff used to talk all the time about you taking him fishing. Man, what I wouldn't have given for a dad to go fishing with." Ralph shook his head, took another sip of beer and continued. "I figured, you know, if I had the pole I could go down to the lake and pretend, maybe hang out with somebody down there or something. I almost, almost had enough, just needed a couple more bucks. Then mom spent too much at the store and I ended up having to use the money to buy gas for her car so she could get to work."

"You poor kid." Austin shook his head. "Did you ever get your fishing pole?"

"Nah, never did." Ralph looked longingly at the small boat parked by the old, beat-up, orange pick-up truck. "Still haven't ever had a chance to go fishing. Always working too much. But man, what I wouldn't give to just one time!"

Austin looked at Ralph. "I'll take you fishing, son."

"Really, you mean it?"

"Yeah." Austin burped. "I love to fish and Geoff never wants to go anymore. I'd love to have someone to go with again."

"Man, you have no idea what that would mean to me." Ralph hugged Austin tight.

"Glad to do it. Glad to do it. Those of us who are on our own gotta look out for each other."

"That we do, that we do," Ralph agreed. "Uh, can I ask a favor, though?"

"What's that?"

"Can we not tell anybody? I mean I'd feel kinda silly having to explain it to people."

"No problem, I understand."

"Man, I gotta get going. It's late."

"Better if you just stay," said Austin. "We gotta get an early start. No one uses the kids' old rooms anyway."

"Yeah, yeah, that's probably better," said Ralph.

Later that night, after he was sure Austin was sound asleep, Ralph crept through the house. He held a flashlight in one hand and his smart phone in the other. As he went from room to room he snapped pictures and made notes.

Andrea was right. The old man had some good stuff lying around.

The next morning Ralph and Austin went fishing like a father and son. They used the beater truck to haul the little fishing boat to the lake. On a nice warm June day they had some competition for good fishing spots. They loaded the supplies and had their poles in the water within an hour. With an open beer in their hand they felt like a day off should.

"Man, you know a fish would sure be good for dinner tonight," said Ralph.

"Well we could catch one if all these idiots on the lake would stop scaring them off."

Ralph looked at the group of rowdy looking red-necks hooting and hollering on their boat while their music blasted. The smallest one looked bigger than him and Austin put together.

"Well, I'd say something to them," said Ralph. "But I hate to spoil our good time."

"You're right, it's just not worth it." Austin shook his head and cast his line. "It's nice to just get out on the lake, even if we don't catch anything."

"It is a beautiful day. I feel kinda bad the others aren't here to enjoy this."

"Don't worry. You were right, they wouldn't appreciate it. And the way the boys behave they'd probably tip over the boat."

"They can get wild. Or well, they used to. I've pretty much put a stop to that."

"Gave them the rubber mallet treatment, did you?"

"Not quite. I just set them straight, explained to them what it meant to be men. I know what it's like growing up without that. I have to say, I think it's having an impact on Andrea and Shelly, too."

"Really?"

"Yeah, I mean they still have their problems but they've really straightened up lately. You should come by and see how different they are."

"I might do that. If I'm welcome, that is. You know just between you and me Ralph what you said hit home. They're all just waiting for me to die to get my goodies."

"Well, I hope it's not that bad, but there is some truth to it."

"My own family. I can't hardly believe it."

"Yeah, ya know I think you're such a nice guy. It's probably hard to give them that tough love they need. I love them all, too, even the boys, they're great boys. But, with my special forces training, I know how to give that tough love. I know in the end they appreciate it more even though it's hard at first."

"That's certainly true." Austin paused and looked at Ralph for a long moment, as if the old man were measuring him with his eyes. "Ralph, I have a confession to make."

"Oh, what's that?"

"Well, I have to tell you, I didn't bring you out here just to take you fishing."

"You didn't?" Oh, God. Ralph hoped the old guy wasn't about to hit on him in the middle of the lake, cause inheritance or not, that was gonna be a deal breaker.

"No, I didn't. I wanted some time to get to know you a little bit more before I asked you for a favor."

"What sort of favor?"

"Well, you know I have to get the trust and power of attorney paperwork finished here soon."

"Yeah, I know." Ralph's heart was beating fast. Almost... he was almost there.

"And anyway, well I still can't find anyone to take care of my affairs if something happens. I was wondering if you might be willing to do it."

Ralph looked shocked. "Man, you got it. I mean I'm happy to do anything to help you out. I might not stay in town after I finish this job, though."

"No problem. It's all revocable at any time. Two signatures and you'd be a free man again."

"Oh, is it?" Ralph got tense. He was gonna have to move fast. "That's good, that's good."

"So this job is going to keep you here for at least what, a year? Eighteen months?"

"Yeah, something like that."

"So why don't we set things to expire in a year? That gives me the time I need and you know you have an out."

"Sure, sounds great. And if Andrea and Shelly have grown up a little by then you can just give it to them directly."

"You know, under your influence, they just might."

"Stranger things have happened," agreed Ralph.

Austin held out his hand. "We have a deal, then?"

"Yes, we do." Ralph shook his hand.

After the sun was starting to go down, the whole day of fishing only brought in one fish. Ralph and Austin didn't care, it was fun just to drink and talk out on the lake. When they got back to the house they washed up and Ralph headed back to Andrea's house on the spruced up motorcycle.

Chapter 8

Suspicious Minds

The next day William went to the diner to do the lunch rush. He was glad it was slow because Riley was at the dentist for tooth work and the tables and booths needed to be cleaned. He started at the front of the diner and wiped down all the booths. Then he scrubbed the bar and built in bars stools. Finally, he made his way around the piano dais, cleaning all four rings of tables as he went. When he came back around he noticed that Geoff had come in and was sitting at the bar. The crazed look on his face was both amusing and disturbing.

"Hey, want a drink?" William asked.

"Later, like at dinner."

"So, why are you sitting at the bar if you don't want to drink?"

"Fine, gimme a beer."

"You coming over to Andrea's tonight?" William asked as he poured the beer.

"I'd like to."

"But, what? You got a hot date tonight?"

"No."

"Didn't think so," William said followed by a laugh.

"Gimme that beer," Geoff said. William handed it to him.

"Really, what's up? You always come over for dinner."

"Andrea and Shelly don't want me around anymore."

"What? Why?"

"I borrowed Andrea's GPS for work this morning."

"And she kicked you out for it?"

"No, it wasn't that. Turned out she didn't have her GPS. Ralph did."

"So?"

"Well, I was messing with it and I somehow pulled up the list of previous destinations. And well remember I said it was a miracle to have a Roger Maris card in a ten condition?"

"Yeah."

"The most recent destination was a place called Wiley's Sports Collectables. Sure enough, they have a Roger Maris rookie card with ten rating that just arrived last week."

"I knew it! I mean why did he have to go with her to feed a cat? It was waste of time. Plus, he hasn't worked, yet had money for high performance parts for his bike."

"Yeah, well she's pissed at me cause I accused Ralph of doing it."

"What? She doesn't think he did it? Even with that proof?"

"Nope, and she doesn't want me to come over anymore until Ralph is gone."

"Maybe you should call the police."

"Andrea and Shelly said if I called the police I would never be welcome over again, not for Christmas or nothing. They would never want to see me again."

"Oh my God. Ya know, it's been weird. It's like anything this guy says they believe and anything he does is okay. Has he paid any rent yet?"

"No, he hasn't and he's hardly helped out."

"Andrea made it seem like he's been scrubbing the house day and night."

"He did a few dishes and swept the porch, that's about it."

"He's over at your dad's house doing tile," William said.

"Yeah, he isn't charging dad at all, but that doesn't really help her or me."

"I'm sorry about Roger being gone."

"Yeah, maybe I'll have a few more drinks," Geoff said as he slammed down the empty mug.

William poured some Bud Light for Geoff with no charge and told him to help himself to the taps while he finished lunch. William worked the shift and checked on Geoff often to make sure he was okay. By the end of the shift Geoff had four beers under his belt and still seemed upset about the mess. With the last customer gone

William went back over to listen to Geoff more.

"I can't decide which is worse," Geoff said. "Losing my sisters or Roger Maris."

"I'll try to talk to them."

"Don't do that. I don't want her to know I came to see you. I don't wanna make it worse."

"This is total bull."

"Yeah," Geoff said as he pulled out a gun from under his shirt.

"Dude!" William yelped.

"What?"

"You carry a God damn gun around?"

"Yep, got my concealed permit. Look at this bad boy," Geoff said. He showed William the brushed nickel with black trim Jericho 9mm handgun. "Israel Military Industries" was engraved on the guns barrel. William hadn't seen a lot of guns, and most of the ones he had seen had been being pointed at him by police officers, but he had to admit Geoff's gun looked a lot nicer than those had been. His only hope was that Geoff carried it around to show people and not to harm anyone.

"Wow, that's sweet," William said.

"Yeah, look at these sights, they're so accurate you could shoot a flea off a horse." Geoff said as he showed William how easily the sights of the gun lined up on a target.

"Those sights are nice. They must really know how to make guns in Israel."

"Yes, those sights are nice," Geoff said. He looked at William for about five seconds with a sinister smile. "Wouldn't Ralphie look nice through those sights?"

"Oh boy," William replied, not knowing how else to respond. He knew Geoff was a reasonable guy and didn't feel too alarmed by his statement. William listened carefully to every word Geoff said from that point on for any indication that there would be bloodshed. He decided that more likely than not Geoff just needed to blow off steam. With one more beer drank Geoff decided to leave. William hoped he wasn't making a mistake by not wanting to tell anyone about their chat.

That evening William decided to go over to Andrea's and see where things stood. To his relief, Ralph didn't seem to be there, but unfortunately Melissa was. She sat at the end of the table making a face that made her look like a constipated frog.

"Hi," said Andrea as William came in.

"Hey," said William. He handed her a box. "I brought salad and some rolls."

"Looks good. Come on in. We're having chili."

"Cool." William took a place at the table.

He was sad not to see Geoff there. He also knew Geoff must be gloomy knowing his own sisters didn't want him over. William didn't know whether to have the chat with the girls, or stay silent and keep his promise to Geoff to not stir up trouble.

The boys sat in their usual places at the center of the table. They looked glassy-eyed and listless. Philip looked like he might even fall asleep.

Andrea served up big bowls of chili along with plates of the salad and rolls William had brought.

"These are stale," Melissa said, poking at a roll with her finger.

"We baked them fresh this morning," said William.

"No, you didn't. Look, they have spots!"

"Those are called 'herbs'."

"They look like mold. It's gross."

"So don't eat them."

"I can't believe you serve moldy food at your diner."

"It is not mold."

"Yes, it is. I'm going to file a complaint."

"Don't you dare! I worked my ass off to get that place going."

"Only dumbasses work. Some of us are smart enough they don't have to work."

"Like you? Yeah real genius you are, mooch off Andrea and your parents yer whole life."

"At least I don't stink like grease all day."

"No, you just stink. Too bad Shelly couldn't smack you and ground you like she did the boys. I see they're actually behaving well today."

"You beat your kids?" Melissa shouted at Shelly.

"I hardly swatted them. They almost broke Ralph's guitar."

"Oh my God," Melissa gasped. "I'm calling you in for child abuse."

"I had to! Do you know how bad I would've felt if they broke his guitar?"

"Doesn't fuckin matter," Melissa roared. "You never hit kids. My parents never hit me, yelled at me or grounded me or anything."

"Yeah," William added, "You're the perfect example of what happens when you have beatniks for parents that let you run wild and free."

"William!" Andrea snapped. "Quit being so rude."

Melissa's phone rang and she answered it. William couldn't decide which was worse, her blabbing on the phone at the table as loud as she could through dinner or her talking to him. She continued to talk on the phone through the whole rest of dinner. William felt like her voice was waterproof, nobody could drown her out.

When dinner finished, Andrea and William wanted to have a few drinks.

"One of us has to take Mel home, maybe we should before we drink too much," Andrea said.

"Make her walk, I'm not taking her," William protested.

"I can't walk," Melissa replied. "A pretty girl like me will get raped if I'm out walking."

William snorted in laughter at her delusion. "Any guy that rapes you better mace himself first," William mumbled softly enough that nobody heard it.

"I'll take her home," Shelly said. "I wanna stop by dad's house with some food for Ralph. All dad ever has to eat is tuna, saltines and cigarettes."

Shelly and Melissa left. The last thing William heard was Melissa saying "I hope nobody I know sees me in your loser-mobile."

William got some wine and cigarettes ready to go. He didn't know where to start as far as talking to Andrea about the people in her life. Relaxation was all that was on his mind and that would be ruined if he spoke of Melissa or Ralph. After having a drink and lighting a cigarette the conversation began.

"So, doesn't Melissa have tons of men that want to have dinner with her?" William started.

"I don't think so."

"Why do you invite Melissa over so much?" William asked.

"She's been my best friend since fifth grade. We're practically sisters."

"But she's an idiot!"

"So's Mitch, but you still hang out with him."

"That's different. Mitch was there for me at the worst times in my life. Never would have made it without him."

"Right, and I've never had hard times and had my friends pull me through?"

William felt that her friends were useless to her when she fell on hard times, but thought it might be better not to say so directly. He focused on a different tactic instead.

"But she's not there for you," he said. "All she does is eat your food and put you down."

"How would you know, William? You're not even here most of the time."

"You're right. I'm running around working all day and trying to make a living."

"Look, I'm sorry, okay?" Andrea said followed by a sigh. "I just don't like feeling like I have to choose between you and my best friend."

"I'm not asking you to. I'm just saying can we see her a little less? She's really annoying sometimes. She can't go five seconds without saying some insult to someone."

"Fine. I won't invite her over when you're here anymore, okay?"

William was baffled by her hostile tone. How had he ended up the bad guy? All was trying to do was look out for her. Well, as long as she was mad at him anyway he figured they might as well deal with the rest of what was bothering him.

"Okay, on to something even more important. What's up with Ralph?" William asked.

"What do you mean?"

"Well he's been here way longer than he said he would. Is everything okay?"

"Yeah, he just didn't start the job yet and has been working for my dad."

"Do the things he does seem odd to you?"

"Like?"

"Ya know, hun, just everything he says, the World Trade Center, the big dark Mexican that walks in shadows, this job he still hasn't started yet, the rent he's not paid to you yet."

"Oh I know, but he's not doing any harm. He's over at my dad's house now working for free. I never thought he would actually pay for the new furnace, but somehow I gotta save up for one come winter."

"Isn't your dad pretty well off financially? Why does he need Ralph to work on the room for free for him?"

"I don't know. Geoff told Ralph he would do the room at the end of the summer. Ralph knows the old man could probably afford to hire someone, but he just doesn't want dad to waste money on something he could easily do."

"Did he say when he plans to leave?"

"No, he didn't."

"How 'bout you set a time limit? Tell him that rain or shine, job or no job he's gotta be gone in two weeks no matter what?"

"I wanna give him at least three."

"Okay three, but I just feel he's overstayed and might not be doing good for you."

"He has done nothing wrong."

William sighed and shook his head. He knew he had to tell about what happened at the diner earlier.

"Look honey," William started. "It's been killing me, did he steal Roger Maris from Geoff."

"Oh geez, Ralph told me about the GPS and Willy's Sports Collectables."

"What?"

"Ralph was actually going there to see about a Whitey Ford card for Geoff's birthday. One in good shape is way out of budget. But me, Shelly and him were all gonna go in on one that was beat up just he could have one."

"Oh really? I think Geoff is convinced otherwise."

"Yeah, I know. Lemme guess, Geoff came crying to you about

how terrible we're treating him?" Andrea said in a heated tone.

"Well, he just said he's not welcome here anymore," William replied to try to calm her down.

"Yeah, well, Geoff pissed me off when he was screaming and accusing Ralph like that. When Ralph was over at the house helping me with the cat he never left my sight. He couldn't have stolen it, I would've noticed. Geoff either lost it, or someone took it. He's just blaming Ralph because he's an easy target."

"Well, are you guys gonna forbid Geoff to ever come over again?"

"When he cools down and can act civil he can come back and see us. He needs to quit pouting about it. I'm not gonna have him interrogating Ralph every time he comes over."

"Alright, sounds good. In three weeks Ralph will be on his own and Geoff hopefully finds the card."

They drifted into an awkward silence. William didn't understand why he couldn't get through to Andrea and make her understand how dangerous Ralph was. He just kept becoming more and more of a wedge between them. It had gotten to the point where even if Ralph left today the damage was done. Anytime either of the girls got mad at him in the future the only thoughts he would have would be "I bet you wouldn't yell at Ralph if he did that" or "if Ralph did it, it would be okay." What was even more depressing was that neither of the girls seemed to care that he was sad and isolated from them.

William finished his drink and left. Andrea didn't bother to say good-bye.

After a few weeks of spending less time with Andrea and more time at the diner William was getting burned out. He had hoped Andrea would ask why he was so distant, but she didn't. Every time he would go see her, Ralph was always there and had become a bigger and bigger influence. He was ready to start calling it "Ralph's house." His phone rang. It was Andrea.

"Hello," William said. It saddened him that he used to want to answer it "hello honey" or "hello babe." Now he answered it like she was a customer or something.

"My dad might be dead!" Andrea cried.

"What happened? What do you mean?"

"Him and Ralph were fixing his fishing boat. They took it out to the lake to test it and dad slipped off and fell in the water. Ralph tried to save him but the water took him away."

"Oh God, really?"

"Yes, none of us know what to do. Please come over tonight."

William called Riley to ask him to finish the dinner shift while he went to go comfort Andrea and family. When he arrived he saw Geoff, Andrea, Shelly and Ralph in the dining room in a heartbreaking mood. William didn't quite know what to do. Now was not the time for suspicious minds. He sat and did his best to comfort them.

"They haven't found a body," Ralph said. "He may be okay."

"What happened, exactly?" William asked.

"We put new heads on the engine of the boat. We went out to the lake to test it and he just slipped and fell right off. I jumped off to chase after him but the current took him away. I even swam back to boat and looked for him but he was gone. Rather than look for him more I went back to shore, called the cops and they got search and rescue out looking for him."

"He's a strong old guy. He can swim, too," Shelly said.

"Yeah, he took swimming lessons since he was like five," Geoff added.

"Oh," Ralph said. "That's good to know."

William noticed a slight expression of panic from Ralph when he learned the old man could swim. Nobody else noticed and now was not the time to try to over analyze this. William decided to do his best to comfort them. For the evening, William forgot the fact that the relationship was in peril and stayed the night with Andrea in his arms.

In the next few days Ralph wasn't around much and even stayed the night somewhere else. William let Riley run the diner for as long as it would take to either find Austin or his body. Everywhere Andrea and Shelly went he went, too. William's suspicions were getting the best of him. He was doing a great job of keeping everyone sane, but he couldn't keep himself sane.

As much as he cared for the girls and even Geoff he felt smothered by their clinginess. Panic washed over him as he imagined the house closing in on him. He couldn't breath. Even if it was just for a little while, he had to get out of there.

Andrea shot him a wounded look as he reached for his keys. William went over and put his arm around her waist.

"I won't be long," he said. He gently kissed her forehead. "I just have to go to the bank and then sign off on the diner's supply order."

"And then you'll be right back?" She asked in a small little girl voice.

"Before you even have time to miss me. Try to relax. I'll bring back something for dinner."

He pulled away from her. She followed him to the door.

"Be careful, okay?"

William smiled. "I always am."

William drove over to Austin's place. He saw the truck and the boat on the trailer parked in the driveway. Since nobody was in sight he went to look over the boat and truck. Snooping around made him feel like a private eye on one of those bad 80's T.V. shows. He didn't even know what he was looking for. He hoped to find something. Luckily, it didn't take much super sleuthing to find a huge clue.

He opened the boat's engine housing. Inside, decades worth of crusty grime covered the motor. There were no tool marks in the caked on grease. The goopy mess around the engine heads was so thick it was unlikely they would have come out at all. While it wasn't exactly a smoking gun, the state of the engine did cast suspicion on Ralph's story.

William hesitated, unsure what to do next. In the end he pulled out his phone and snapped a few pictures of the engine and its filthy, worn-out heads. He had no idea what to do with the pictures, but taking them at least made him feel like he had accomplished something.

His phone beeped in his hand. A text message from Andrea appeared.

"Hurry home. Xox," it read.

William sighed. He wanted to look around some more, but obviously he couldn't be gone much longer. He'd have to come back later.

Halfway to Andrea's he remembered his promise to bring home

something for dinner. Swearing to himself, he pulled into the nearest drive-through and ordered a bucket of fried chicken along with a couple of side dishes.

"Hail the conquering hero," he muttered to himself as he dropped the food onto the passenger seat beside him. At least he could still occasionally do something right.

When he came in the front door he noticed the mood at Andrea's seemed even gloomier than it had before he left. A heavy, funeral-like silence hung over the table while they ate.

"Good chicken," Geoff said.

"Thank you, but I didn't make it, the Colonel did," William replied.

They lapsed into another silence. After what seemed like hours, Andrea finally broke it.

"The head of Search and Rescue came by while you were gone." She pushed an uneaten chicken leg back and forth on her plate with a fork as she spoke. "He said if they don't find something by tomorrow they're going to call off the search."

"Doesn't matter," William said. He tried to sound more confident than he felt. "If anything, not finding a body right away makes it more likely he's alive somewhere."

"But what if we never find him? I don't think I could stand not knowing what happened. "

William took her hand. "I'll talk to them, okay? Between the taxes on the diner and the contribution I made at their annual fundraiser I practically paid for that whole squad myself. The least they can do is give you a few extra days."

Andrea nodded, but she kept staring at her plate with a completely blank expression on her face. William had never felt more helpless.

The next day William went back to Austin's. At first glance nothing looked different, then he noticed the front door was partially open. After debating with himself for a bit he decided to go in the house. He found Ralph in living room, wearing Austin's old blue terrycloth bathrobe.

"What are you doing here?" Ralph asked.

"Funny, I was about to ask you the same thing," said William.

"Me? I'm trying to make sure sense out of this fucking mess, man. That's what I'm doing here. Austin's lawyer called last me last night. Apparently the old man granted me power of attorney. Looks like I'm responsible for his stuff 'til we find him."

"Bullshit!" William said as he threw an old wooden chair in Ralph's general direction. It shattered into pieces when it hit the ground.

"What do you mean? I don't want any of this stuff. It's more of a headache. I got big jobs and contracts to worry about. His house and truck and boat is peanuts compared to what I got coming to me. I got a two hundred grand a year job coming. This is all more pain than it's worth to me."

"Oh yeah, at Acme Construction, 'meep meep.' There is no such company. Also, I looked up all the contractors for the World Trade Center. You were not listed as contributing to it at all. I know you stole that girl's C.D. case and pretended you fought Antonio Banderas for it back. I know you stole Geoff's Roger Maris card. Now you killed her father for his money."

"That is just ridiculous!"

"Really? Why are the heads so dirty on the boat engine? You said you guys just replaced them."

"Oh my God, William! That's not the boat we took out. The police impounded that. He picked up that piece of shit on the back of the truck at an estate sale."

"Really? I got a few friends in the police department. Maybe I'll ask them where Austin's boat is?"

"This is so selfish of you. Andrea and Shelly are on the verge of a nervous breakdown and you wanna play this?

"Play what? What happened to Geoff's card?"

"Geoff probably never had the card. He just wanted an insurance settlement."

"Meep, meep."

"Funny, William. Look, Acme Construction is a decoy. The company I work for does top secret construction. We do underground bunkers for political figures. We even did secret defense system for the new World Trade Center. I can't tell their real name. The trucks are not marked and we can't talk to anyone about what we do."

"Your nose is gonna poke me in the face, Pinocchio."

"Whatever. Please don't stress the girls out more, okay? Once they settle down, I'll divide up dad's stuff fairly like he wanted me to."

"You're a fraud, you're goin' down. Andrea is gonna throw you sky high outta her house when she hears what you've done."

"Don't hurt them more, William!" Ralph called out as William walked towards his car.

He started the car and revved the engine. As he pulled away, a dirt cloud was left in his wake. Not knowing what to do, he decided to go back to Andrea's house. His cell phone rang. The caller I.D. showed it was Mitch. At first he didn't want to answer it because he figured Mitch would just go on and on about some nonsense. Since Mitch knew what was going on, he answered it just in case it was any news about Austin."Yeah," William answered.

"We live in a hick town, ya know that?"

"Man, I'm like in a crisis here! I'm gonna have to take a rain check on whatever is pissing you off today."

"No man, I mean this will help you. A few days ago a truck dropped off this derelict to the hospital. He had a head wound and no ID. He reeked of alcohol and they thought it was just another drunk that feel down and hurt himself. He didn't even know who he was. He was like smelly, dirty and wet. I think it's daddy. He woke up today and keeps asking for his kids, Shelly and Andrea and Geoff."

Chapter 9

Beyond Reasonable Doubt

William pulled the car over, slammed the brakes and left skid marks on the road. The tires screeched as he turned around to head to he hospital. Several cars beeped at him, but William couldn't care less. Even with the phone in one hand, a cigarette in the other he still managed to drive properly.

"What do you mean he had a head wound?" William asked.

"Yeah, big old gash across the back of his head and some bruising on his front temples. The doctor's report said he was knocked unconscious and had hypothermia. They found a decent amount of alcohol in his blood."

"Okay, I'm on the way."

"See ya soon."

William called Andrea and arrived at the hospital before the others did. William found Mitch and they headed to the room. A sergeant from the rescue crew was in the room waiting for William.

"It's that the man we been looking for all week?" The sergeant asked.

"Yep."

"Okay then, I'll tell the boys to call off the search," The sergeant said and then left the room.

"Next time there's a missing person, try the hospital first," William called after him.

"Hey Mitch," William said. "I've lost all respect for the city's government and search and rescue. They spent all that time and money and person they were looking for almost a week was in the hospital the whole time."

"I know. Bunch of morons."

Austin was awake and recognized William. Before asking any questions, William decided to let the old man eat some dinner. He went out into the hallway with Mitch.

"Mitch, This Ralph guy, he did this I know it."

"You've said it, but why? There's no motive."

"He convinced the old guy to make him executor of the will. Ralph is living at his house right now as we speak. I mean Ralph gets to decide who gets what and controls all of Austin's assets. He was bragging about it at dinner last week. I knew there was something to that look on his face when he said if he was in charge he'd be fair."

"Maybe we should get the police involved."

"We might. Andrea and Shelly are on the way. We'll see what they say."

Andrea and Shelly arrived shortly. William could see their pain and suffering wash away as they saw John Doe was their father. Tears of joy were shed from both of them to see their dad had been safe all week.

"Oh man, what happened to me?" Austin asked.

"I had hoped you would remember," William said.

"Me and Ralph were on the lake."

"Testing the boat's new engine?" William asked.

"Ahh, no, just fishing. We've been going for weeks now."

"Then what?"

"I don't know! I think something hit my head. I remember Ralph saying something like 'sorry pops' or something like that. Then, I was really dizzy and fell in the water. I swam to shore and passed out. I guess these guys threw me in the back of their truck and drove me to the hospital."

"Was it possible you hit a rock when you fell into the water?"

"No, whatever I hit was on the boat."

William decided to stop his interrogation and let Austin and his daughters have bonding time. He and Mitch went out to the hallway. They waited till the girls were done seeing dad and met them in the hall.

"See, Ralph lied. He said they were testing a new engine, but they weren't. And what's this 'sorry pops' comment all about?" William said.

"Yeah," Mitch added. "How could he have hit his head on something in the boat?"

"I think Ralph is a serious liar. I think he's responsible for this," William said.

"What?" Shelly demanded.

"Did you know he's at your dad's house and has control over all of his affairs?"

"Yes, he told us. I told him that dad was okay. He's on his way over."

"Oh my God," William said. "This man is in danger. Mitch, this room needs to be guarded twenty-four hours a day. Can you do that?"

"Yeah, no problem, William."

"What are you doing?" Andrea asked.

"Protecting your dad. Ralph lied about fixing the boat, he was alone with your dad when he fell, he said a weird comment, and with your dad out of the picture Ralph gains control of all his money. It's pretty conclusive he tried to kill you dad for money. He might come back to finish the job. Do you think we should call the police? I mean, he's at your dad's house now so he'll be easy to catch. You could bag up his stuff and store it or something. Just get it out of your house."

"Do not call the police," Andrea snapped.

"Yeah, what the fuck?" Shelly added.

"You don't wanna have him arrested for this?"

"For what? My dad probably slipped. I'm not going to be mad at Ralph 'cause my dad's clumsy," Andrea stated.

"Clumsy? Ralph had motive, means and opportunity. I mean, you really don't think this is foul?"

"I'm not gonna try to get him put in jail."

"Yeah," Shelly added. "Dad's okay. We don't need to bring Ralph down. He's a really great guy. I don't wanna see him go to jail."

"Are you at least going to throw him out?"

"No, I don't want him to leave," Andrea said.

"Where would he go?" Shelly added.

William brushed his hands through his hair. The fact that they wanted to let Ralph completely walk for all the things he had done made him livid. He looked at them and just shook his head. Ralph was truly untouchable. Nothing he said was going to get through to him. The once decent relationship he had was now at it's conclusion.

"I can't deal with this anymore. Since Ralph is like the king of kings go get him. You both can spend the rest of your life serving him."

"You're mad because my dad put Ralph in charge?" Andrea stated. "Why would you care?"

"Because he's gonna hold you for ransom over your own inheritance. I mean, if Austin had died he would decide how much or how little you get."

"Look, dad's okay and Ralph said he would be fair."

"Yeah, I'm sure he would've been real fair. As long as you guys take turns sucking his cock, he'll throw you a dollar or two of your own money now and again. It's just amazing how untouchable this guy is. Can he do no wrong?"

"That's enough William, I've had it with this."

"Me, too," he replied as he walked away. It seemed like hours as he walked down the hallway alone to the parking lot. He drove away in a slow and disappointed manner. The only two choices before him were to put up with Ralph being emperor of their world or walk away and leave forever. Not really sure what the right choice was, he went for a long drive like he always loved to do. The nice summer breeze and low traffic made his trip to nowhere very pleasurable.

He didn't know whether to be mad at them for pushing him away, or be concerned that Ralph would probably clean them out financially and emotionally. An image of them smiling and giggling as they listened to Ralph made him think he shouldn't care about them.

After a whole tank of gas was burned, he went home. By the front door were three garbage bags full of his clothes and stuff he kept at Andrea's house. He brought the bags in the house and sorted them out. Some of the items had never even been in his personal home because they were bought when he was with Andrea and stayed at her house.

Even though he knew it was coming to this sooner or later, it was going to be a long hard night. The situation reminded him of a family member dying of cancer. When the day comes when they actually die it is still a hard pill to swallow. Like always, he convinced himself he would be alright, but he knew sorrow would creep up on him fast. All he could do is try to keep his mind focused on something else.

The next day after the lunch and dinner shifts were done he got his usual drinks and decided to start writing on the computer. At first he wrote gibberish, but then he decided to write a short story. He got so involved in his writing that he drank way too much and stayed up till 5 A.M. The sun was coming up and he decided to sleep and let Riley take over lunch.

As time went on he kept a rigorous schedule. He would work as much as he could, write his story, and drink Gentleman Jack all night. Work didn't seem as bad as it did when he had a relationship. He didn't have to worry about what time it was or relying on Riley to run dinner shift by himself. He noticed he enjoyed socializing with his bar customers more, a job Riley used to do.

"What'll be?" William asked a well dressed senior pilot. The man's clean shaven face and crew cut showed a great deal of professionalism. William didn't expect this guy to be a big drinker since he looked very healthy for a guy pushing sixty. The man sat down and looked at the many bottles on the shelf. After a few moments he decided.

"Johnny Walker, straight up."

"You got it." William poured the drink and saw the man's airline company credit card.

"You get free drinks from your company?"

"Yep. That's what you get for thirty-five years of service. I'm Captain Harry Ordway."

"Well Captain Ordway, I can just leave the bottle if you like. Welcome to our city."

"Thanks. I land here a lot. Mostly private flights. I live in Sunnyvale. Anything fun to do in this town?"

William snorted in laughter "Haven't found anything fun yet. There's a whore house a few blocks from here."

"No thanks. I got a wife and kids, don't need that garbage."

"Good for you."

"Yeah, my oldest one is going into the Navy and my youngest made captain of the debate team. Been married thirty-five years."

Harry said and quickly guzzled down another shot of whiskey.

"Wow, a charmed life, huh? Your wife didn't dump you for some shyster con artist with a guitar?"

"Well, I had a rough start. When I was a teen I stole a slot machine from this mafia kingpin named Joey."

"Oh, shit."

"Yeah, he was gonna kill me, but instead he had me help him collect old debts from his partner that ripped him off. Then I helped Joey fake his death to escape his gangster lifestyle."

"Really?"

"Yeah, I mean this guy could collect debts owed to him. There's only three things guaranteed in this life; taxes, death and if you owe Joey money, yer payin' it."

"Joey should work here. I have a whole stack of bad checks I got. I only collect about sixty percent of the.. The rest I gotta eat. "

"Joey never had bad checks written at his casino. An I.O.U. to Joey was as good as cash. Ya know what Joey's debt collection success rate was?

"What?"

"One hundred percent. You know what happens if you didn't pay Joey his money?"

"He'd kill ya with a soldering iron?"

"I don't know. Nobody- including me- has ever not paid him. I wish I'd've bought stock in D-O-J. Debts owed to Joey. It's the only stock with a one hundred percent guaranteed return." Harry continued to drink more on his company account.

"You know his enemy Frank thought he could rip Joey off. He just had the attitude that, nobody could hurt him." Harry paused and stared directly at William with an aloof cold expression on his drunken face. The stare lasted a good ten seconds. William got a bit disturbed by Harry's dramatic expression.

"I think he was wrong," Harry continued and stopped staring at William.

After an hour of slamming shots William was certain Harry was highly intoxicated. William knew there was a liability if Harry caused an accident because of being over served at the diner. Just as Riley was about to demand Harry's car keys he saw a taxi driver come into the diner looking for Harry to take him to a hotel. William breathed in relief, charged the account and had Harry sign off on it.

"Here you go. If the company doesn't pay it I'm gonna have Joey track you down," William said.

"Oh man, it'll be paid. I mean if you owe Joey money, yer fuckin' paying it! You're fuckin' payin' it," Harry continued and waved his arms in an aggressive motion.

"I'll keep that in mind," William said. He chuckled to himself and had an idea that it would be funny if Ralph had borrowed or stolen money from this Joey and hadn't paid it back. The thought turned foul when he realized if someone tried to kill Ralph, Andrea and Shelly would probably throw themselves in front of Ralph to take the bullet. After Harry left in the taxi William spoke with Riley. They agreed that the Joey stories were funny.

"Is this what I've been missing not working dinner shift?" William asked.

"Yeah, pretty much," Riley replied.

Mitch came into the diner to hang out for awhile. The three of them chatted until it was time to close. William enjoyed top shelf whiskey while Mitch drank four Mike's Hard Lemonades. Riley did the Z out's and William helped the cook close down the kitchen. When all the work was done the employees and Mitch went home. Afterward a puzzled look came to William's face.

"Did Mitch pay for those beers?" William asked.

"Does he ever? He's going to the Love House tonight."

"Oh my God. Gotta love the whore house. It's the only place where all men are truly created equal. I'm sending Joey after his ass."

"Yeah, good luck with that."

"I think that should be Moe's Diner's new motto. I'm tired of bounced checks. You owe Moe's Diner money, yer paying it," William said and pointed his finger at Riley. After Riley left he went to work on his story and drinking Gentleman Jack. It seemed that the words came together easily and a once short story was becoming a real novel. With some self control only a few shots were drank and he was in his bed before sunrise.

For some reason the dinner the next evening was sluggish. William and Riley stood around until an older man who was clean shaven with black slicked-back hair and short, stocky body sat at the bar. He wore dark blue suit and tie that seemed more suited to an accounting office than a night out at a bar. It didn't take long to see the badge on his breast pocket that exhibited he was an agent with the F.B.I. William's alarm rose until the man just asked for some vodka.

"Here you go. You sure you don't want some tonic with that?" William asked.

"Nope, just plain straight up vodka for me tonight."

"Cool, couldn't help noticing you're I.D. F.B.I., huh?"

"Yep, I'm Agent Jack Reddick. I'm new to this branch."

"What brings you here?"

"I'm from Utah. I was a police sergeant out there for years till I got in with the bureau. My second wife got a job out here so I transferred."

"Second wife, huh?"

"It's sort of a long story."

"What, the first one left ya for some long haired hoodwinker?"

"No, she was murdered in Utah," Jack replied as he finished his first shot.

"What?" William said embarrassed at his previous comment. "Here this one's on the house," he continued and handed Jack a second shot. "What happened?"

"She was a marriage counselor. The husband of one of her clients tracked her down and shot her right at the middle school. He blamed her for his divorce."

"Oh yeah, I heard about that. I remember now. He and his accomplice got executed, didn't they?"

"Yep, firing squad."

The two spoke longer. It was getting easier for William to converse with his customers. Usually, he just wanted them to drink and get out. Now he actually really cared what they had to say. A debate went on in his mind if it was good that he enjoyed socializing with bar people or if it meant he was desperate for stories of other people's pain. Jack left and William got ready to close. Mitch decided to come in and sit at the closed bar.

"Come to mooch some more beer?" William said.

"Who's mooching? I earn it. So, William, what are you gonna do after work now?" Mitch asked.

"Go write some more."

"What are you writing?"

"Just a short story."

"Why?"

"Cause I want to."

"Can I see it?"

"Never show a work in progress."

"Oh, come on, you should go to the Love House sometime."

"I don't know about that. I think I've seen enough crack whores in my life."

"Come on, yer single now. Try it sometime, you'll love it. And, you'll be supporting local business."

"I'll think about it," William replied as he did the last of the closing duties.

Chapter 10

Confidante

After Mitch left William went back to writing his story. For some reason he was having writer's block. No matter how much he drank or smoked the ideas just were not flowing. A quick thought came upon him to go to the Love House. It didn't take long to dismiss the idea. The thought came back and this time he grabbed his keys and went to his car.

"It's a good idea to check out local business- see how other places are doing in town," He said to himself as he drove away.

The neon sign nearly blinded him as he drove to the end of a commercial block. Buried away at the end of a dark street was the not-so-secret Love House. Luckily, it was slow and only a few cars were in the lot as he parked. He felt the jitters as he got out and approached the building. A quick thought that he should go back home vanished as quickly as it appeared.

He opened the glass front door and entered a small foyer where a thick locked metal door prevented anyone from going further. A small sign said "Ring doorbell and ladies will answer. Please give them time." With a shaking hand he rang the doorbell. While he waited, he looked around the small foyer and saw posters of naked models. All of the business licensing and affiliations were posted in plain view.

This place was a member of the Rotary Club and the Better Business Bureau. They also had certificates that acknowledged they donated money to the county safe house for battered women, the Fraternal Order of Police and the same New Laws program that William was persecuted by Roger for donating to. An attractive girl in sparkling bra and panties answered the door.

"Well, hello there," She said with a smile. "Come on in. Ever been here before?"

"No, I haven't."

"Who are you and what do you do?"

"I'm William. I own the diner a few blocks from here."

"Right this way."

William was about to just ask her for directions on how to get out of there. Instead, he decided to give it a chance. For a moment he felt like a jerk for the fact that he was nervous about being in a place that most normal guys would love to be in. He didn't know if his lack of cat calls and hooting and hollering made the girl edgy. He didn't know if she liked someone polite or wanted to be objectified. It was assumed that most guys came in and instantly started to say perverted things to the girls.

The place had tiger print carpet throughout. They walked down the hallway and he saw several attractive half-naked girls who smiled at him as he went by. They made it to one of the private rooms. There was a zebra print sofa for him to sit down on. The room was covered in mirrors and in the middle was a stage. The pole in the middle of the stage was clear with water bubbles going through it. A quick glace around showed towels, lotions, dirty magazines and porno movies playing silently on a TV hanging off the wall.

"So which model do you want to see?" The girl asked.

"Umm, I really didn't have anyone special in mind."

"Well, how about Cherry? She's real nice."

"Okay, Cherry it is."

"Okay. Get comfortable and I'll go get her."

William peeked at the movie on the T.V. After watching it a few minutes he laughed at what he could comprehend of the storyline. A black hit man broke into a beautiful girl's apartment ready to shoot her dead. Without sound it was hard to know exactly how in only a few minutes they ended up having sex in the living room instead of her being murdered. By the end the girl handed him his gun that he dropped in the passion of sexual gratification.

"Hi, William, I'm Cherry," a girl's voice said.

William gasped as she came in. Cherry was almost as tall as he was with long shiny blond hair. Her baby blue eyes sparkled along with a perfect smile. Her healthy hourglass figure made her tight clothes look pleasant for him. She had to be five to ten years older than him and twenty years older than the girl who answered the door. Still, she had a more natural and attractive appearance than the door girl.

She walked by William and sat down. It was unexplainable why the young hot girl at the door along with the others in the hall didn't make him feel as lovely as she did. He slightly stared at her for a moment. William wondered if she thought her big breasts hanging out or the tight camel toe in her panties was all he liked about her. Although those features were just fine with him, something about her just put him on cloud nine. She seemed ethereal, almost angelic, like she had stepped into the room out of his dreams.

It was as if he could cry in her arms if he wanted to without humiliation. She put her arm around him and all the years of frustration, anger, and grief from the wars he'd fought just fell away from him. No matter how hard he tried he couldn't stop feeling like a little kid in candy store. This was not the type of girl he would've ever imagined being here.

"So what do you wanna do? I just want to say I don't suck anything or have sexual intercourse," She stated.

"Well, I have the one idea I sure wouldn't mind trying."

"Do tell," She said with a smile.

He explained what his idea was and was staggered that she didn't think it was too bad. Even though it was her job to please the gentlemen that came in, she looked as if she genuinely enjoyed making men happy. The other girls probably hated men and just want their damn money as fast as they could get it. It wasn't in a whorish way, but instead Cherry seemed like she understood and saw nothing wrong with the fact that men needed sexual outlets. She was glad to give them what the outside world was not giving them.

Afterward William left the club with a good wholesome feeling. The things they did were not to taboo at all. Even though he was wowed by her, he was glad she wasn't the type that would go all the way with a guy for a fee. He got to have fun, support local business, and see Cherry. The hope was that Cherry was a stage name and that her parents were not mean enough to name her that.

The next evening Mitch came in again and William told of his trip to the Love House.

"Finally, huh? Wasn't it great?"

"Yeah, the girl Cherry was very nice."

"Man, we should go together sometime and trick Riley into coming."

"I don't think that's Riley's thing."

"We'll tell him we're gonna go look at an engine that gets one hundred miles to a gallon."

"Yeah, he'll love that."

Later on the crowd got busy and William had to help wait tables. Mitch stayed at the bar and drank a beer. Coming out of the kitchen with a tray of food in his hand William saw a familiar girl at the bar. Quickly he jolted back into the kitchen to avoid being seen. The food fell off the tray and crashed to the ground. The cook decided to just redo the order and ask what happened later.

"Piss. Dammit!" William yelped.

The noise made the girl at the bar look over, but he was out of sight before she could see him. Mitch couldn't help but laugh. William didn't know what to do so he swept up the mess and told the cook he slipped on some water. It was obvious that standing around all night debating what to do was not an option. He would either have to face what was out there or go hide in the office.

"Riley, you see who's at the bar?"

"Yeah, it's Julie Casner."

"Think she knows whose place she's in?"

"I don't know. I'll serve her. Just try not to be seen."

"Either she doesn't know I'm here or she's got a bomb under her shirt and came to blow the place up."

"I'm gonna vote on the first one. Just don't look at her. I'll take care of her."

"Okay, but be careful in case I'm right and her boobs are actually bombs."

William took the other door to the dining room and didn't look over at Julie Casner. It seemed fair to think she had no idea whose diner she was in. Even though Mitch sat two seats down from her, she didn't recognize that he was the guy that creeped her out at a club years ago. Riley approached her just like any other customer. She smiled at him and was happy to be there.

"What'll it be?"

"We're going to have two Long Island iced teas."

"We? Who ya waitin' for?"

"Oh, my husband William."

"William?"

"Yes, here he is."

A thin built man came and sat next to her. He had a classy goatee and long straight hair. He wore slacks along with a maroon vest and tie. This William spoke in an upper class accent and had an intellectual demeanor. Riley made the drinks and tried not to look excited to tell his William what Julie's husband's name was. The drinks were made and Riley spoke with Mitch further down the bar.

"She doesn't recognize me," Mitch said.

"Why would she recognize some guy that freaked her out at a club fourteen years ago?"

"I bet if I start talkin' about Ted Bundy again, she'll remember me."

"Yeah, how bout ya don't?"

"I'm just tryin' to educate."

"Zip it," Riley said sternly as he went back to Julie and her William.

"So, what brings you folks to Moe's Diner?"

"We heard about the place," William said. "It used to be a dump, but now it's pretty trendy."

"Yeah," Julie added. "The place looks great and I heard the food is fantastic."

"Yep, new management really turned this place around."

"Who bought it?" Julie wondered.

"I did, I'm Riley Rosagalio."

"Well," William said. "A very fine job you did redoing this place."

"Thanks, glad to have you here."

William Defreno did a fine job of not being seen by Julie and her William. Even though thinking of Julie brought back memories of his personal war with the Casners, his mind was occupied with thoughts of Cherry. It seemed that his infatuation with her should have worn off by now, but the way she made him feel lasted on. After a few Long Island iced teas Julie and William were about ready to leave.

William Defreno used the bathroom. As he left, he bumped right into Julie. He had no clue she was using the other bathroom at the same time. Julie glanced at William for a moment. He gasped and shook his head. What are the odds, he wondered to himself.

"Piss!" William said.

"I'm sorry sir, I didn't mean to bump into you," Julie said as she walked away.

William watched them leave in a state of puzzlement. How come she didn't remember who he was? He watched out the window as they pulled into the gas station across the street and parked right next the memorial bench with Annie's name on it. "I wonder if they'll notice?" William said to Riley as he walked up to join William at the window.

"They walked right past it."

"You did poison their drinks, right?"

"Ya know, I spoke with them for a little while. I don't think she has clue about you or Annie or anything. I think she still thinks you're dead or never knew about any of the war. I think she just has no clue about anything. If you came and sat down next to them they probably wouldn't know you from Adam."

"I guess so. She didn't even seem like she knew me at all when she ran into me on the way to the bathroom."

"William, you're not public enemy number one anymore. I mean you had your fifteen minutes of fame twice, but it was so long ago."

"I guess so. The world moved on. I think I'm better off being forgotten about."

"Yeah, I didn't want to tell you, but it was becoming pretty narcissistic to think you're still the dinner topic for everyone in town."

That evening William closed the diner and went back to work on his story. Tonight the juices were flowing well, but he still thought about Cherry. A debate went on in his mind whether it was pleasurable or pathetic to have such have a weakness for a girl at The Love House. More and more of his story came together, but a sudden decision to take a break and go see Cherry was made.

This time he wasn't so nervous and Cherry came to his private room fast. After they had their fun, he explained about himself owning the diner and what happened in his relationship. He even told a little about the war with the Casners and Annie being killed at the gas station. Cherry showed an interest in his stories.

"Oh and also Ralph said that this like dark Mexican tried to steal the neighbor girl's C.D. case," William said.

"A dark Mexican, huh?"

"Not dark skinned. Dark because he always walked in shadows. The light just seemed to get out of his way."

"Oh, I see. Sounds terrible."

"Yeah, right. Ralph stole the damn C.D. case and made that up thinking she would like sleep with him or something."

"Did the girl fall for it?"

"No she didn't, but Andrea and Shelly sure did."

"He sounds like this Ralph that used to come in the cabaret I worked at."

"Really?"

"Yeah, he got banned for life. I think his name was Ralph Oats."

"What!" William yelled out. "That's him! Why did he get thrown out?"

"He came in once and ordered a two hundred dollar bottle of Dom Pérignon champagne. All the girls sat with him and drank it. He though he was so cool. Then when it came time to pay he didn't have enough money and settled the bottle for sixty bucks."

"Yeah, that sounds like him."

"Oh then he came back and did it again. The owner told him there would never be a third time cause he was banned from the place."

"I'm not surprised one bit."

"Well, sadly our time is up, but do come back and see me again," Cherry said as she showed him towards the door.

"What nights are you here?"

"It varies. Just look for my white Land Rover in the lot. You'll know I'm here."

"Oh, is that white Land Rover yours?" William asked as they walked from the room to the front metal door.

139

"Yeah, why?"

"Oh man, this big Mexican, I mean big a shit, tried to steal it. He was scary. I couldn't see his face cause the moonlight was too scared and got out of his way, but I got him. He ran off," William said in teasing manner.

"Aww, thank you," Cherry replied as she hugged him.

She unlocked the door and let William out. Once again she left a magnificent experience in his memory. On the way back to the diner he couldn't help but laugh to himself at the scenario he told her. He wrote some more of his story and headed to bed.

A week later he woke up feeling sick and tired. It wasn't from too much drinking the night before. He didn't feel like doing anything today. Riley agreed to do the lunch and dinner shift. He got in his car and drove around aimlessly like he always used to do. The reason for such an isolated feeling was not known to him. The only thing that it could be was that he was pretty much done writing his short story.

Like the trauma he had been through before, once the shock had worn off hard reality set in. It was the same feeling of getting out of a hot bath in the cold. At first the body is still warm, but it wears off fast. All the thrills and new freedom from being single had worn off and the reality of what life was like in the present hit him like a hurricane. It was clear this would not be something that would wear off anytime soon. He drove around on the long highway with nowhere to go.

The sky was covered in gray clouds and weather was nice and cool. After he came back closer to home he drove around the entire city listening to his C.D.s and smoking. Finally, he stopped for gas at the station where Annie had been shot. He looked at memorial bench. With no cares or worries he sat on it and just watched the world go by. He could imagine Annie sitting next to him.

Normally he would be worried about people thinking it was weird that he was sitting on the bench looking at traffic go by. Today it didn't matter one bit and it felt good for him not to care. He smoked and just watched the road some more with a defeated look on his face. It wasn't about winning a war this time or defeating a foe. At least when all it was about was getting the not guilty verdict or getting

Timmy put away there was reason for hope.

The constant thought through his young fighting years was once he beat Timmy and the Casners everything would be fine. This time there was no easy solution. He had to accept that life sucked even after winning his wars. It seemed that writing his short story was the only hope he had and with it finished there was nothing left. This was beyond mid-life crisis or a case of the blues or even treatable depression. This was his Waterloo.

After another few hours the sun began to set. He smiled and watched the sun go down from the bench. As it got darker and darker his nonchalant attitude didn't fade. His rear end was numb from sitting on the bench so long, but he wanted to watch the sun completely set before leaving. Finally he left the bench when dusk was complete and went to check on the diner.

Chapter 11

Midnight Confession

Riley was handling things just fine and figured William just needed a day off. This attitude continued into the weeks ahead just as he thought it would. Since William had become older it seemed harder and harder to just bounce back and grab life by the horns again. Riley became concerned at William's detached behavior. The diner was slipping again and he wanted to fix whatever was wrong before too much damage was done. Finally he decided to ask what was up.

William was hesitant to tell the truth because Riley and Mitch would just say he should go to the Love House more or find a new girl or something. It would be hard to explain that it wasn't about just meeting someone new or getting laid. Rather than even try to explain, William just blamed his absence on being too engaged in writing. It was getting harder and harder to use that excuse, though.

"You know, Riley, a small publisher has decided to publish my short story."

"Really? Well, that's nice. I guess you'll be in a better mood once you're a business owner and an author."

"Well, it's going to be in a big book of short stories. I think like ten others will be in the book."

"Cool. You never did tell me and Mitch what it was about."

"Oh, you'll see when it's published."

"What is this like top secret, like the Masons or something?"

"Yes."

"Well, can I at least know the title?"

"Sure, it's called 'One More Year'."

"Oh really? Well you been kinda out of it since you finished it."

"Oh, I know, I just, uh, well, now I'm bored at night, cause I don't have anything to write."

"Ever tried sleeping at night?"

"Yeah, but I just didn't like it"

"You know Roger Delahoy is going on trial soon. He pled not guilty to the threatening letter he left on your car."

"Oh, well it's not even that serious is it?"

"It is actually. He could go to jail for it."

"Oh my God! Ya know September is only two months away. He could've been training and trying to break it again instead of annoying me and smokin' pot," William stated.

The feeling of becoming Randy Casner was already killing him, but now knowing Roger might get put away for something he didn't do made him feel worse. He felt like he couldn't win. If he was successful he was a bastard in everyone's eyes, yet when he was a loser he was a loser to everyone. It seemed to him that both lifestyles were garbage.

Over the next week he did his best not to let his piss poor attitude show. Even though the diner had been raking in the money over the past few weeks it just didn't matter to him. He knew Riley was bothered by the fact that William quickly changed the subject every time he was asked about his story.

After a miserable July 4th William was happy the holiday and fireworks were over. Every event seems to put him more and more in the doldrums. Most years he was like a little kid lighting off fireworks and loving the booms and noises. The fact that he counted down the hours 'til it was over made him feel like he really had gone to hell. After the diner closed he kicked back a few brew-ha-ha's for the fun of it.

A few turned into a little too much and he started to get uninterested in staying home. Even though he had been drinking he was oblivious to the fact that he shouldn't be driving. Luckily, the place he wanted to go was close and he was a sharp-eyed driver that could still operate just fine. He approached the Love House and saw the white Land Rover that belonged to Cherry was there.

"Come on in," The girl at the door said. "You are here to see

Cherry, huh?"

"Yeah,"

"Ever thought about seeing a different girl?"

"Cherry knows what I like," William replied.

"I bet I know, too," She replied as and kissed his cheek.

She left to find his girl while he waited on the zebra print sofa. He knew that the girl at the door could do the same things Cherry could, but he didn't want to have to explain that she just didn't recharge his soul like Cherry did. While waiting, the thought of what was so great about Cherry came to him. There was no scientific way of explaining why this one and only girl just made him feel so safe and secure and the others didn't. It wasn't that the other girls were rude, pushy or impatient, but they just didn't possess the same spark.

"Well hello, William. Back again, huh?" Cherry said as she came in.

"Oh, yeah."

"How's the diner?"

"Great, we made more these last couple weeks then the whole month of May."

"That's good, I've missed you."

"Yep, I sure am, like ya know, yeah," he replied nervously.

"Huh? What? Are you nervous?"

"Nope, I am, I mean yeah I am."

"Oh, nervous about what were gonna do tonight?"

"Well, actually it's because I been writing and a publisher agreed to publish my short story in a big book of short stories."

"Oh wow, the money will come flying in, huh?"

"You don't make much being an author. I certainly didn't do it for the money."

"Why you nervous about that? You've been famous before."

"Well it's just what the story is about, that's all," William replied.

He was ready to just drop the subject and move on to exciting things they did. He tried to just smile and the feeling of being safe was in the air. Mentioning his book put him in an uneasy state of mind. Not only could he not talk right, but he couldn't even sit still. He figured she would want to know more about it or at least why he was acting so unusual.

"What's it called?" Cherry said. She seemed genuinely interested in his work.

"It's called 'One More Year.'"

"That's an interesting title."

"Yeah, it goes along with the plot."

"What's it about?"

William took a deep breath. Part of him wished she didn't care. The combination of a little too much to drink and the overwhelming glow that came from her made him feel like he could bare his soul to her. He laughed to himself to try to distract his thoughts. She would make a great detective. If he had robbed a bank he would probably confess to her. For whatever reason, he spilled the truth.

"It's about a fella who decides he's had enough in life. So, the 'One More Year' is like a bucket list of things he could realistically do. After his bucket list is complete he's ready for that hit between the eyes."

"So basically he does all the fun things he always wanted to do and then he's going to shoot himself?"

"Yeah, that's why the title is 'One More Year.' For one year he does all the things he wanted to do."

"Hmm, what gave you the idea? Is it based on anything real?"

"Well, not yet. Right now it's fiction. Once it's published it will become non fiction."

"You mean like it's about you?" She said in a troubled tone.

"Well, it's egotistical to write about yourself, but yeah it's basically based off me."

"When do I get to read it?" She asked with one raised eyebrow

"Well, it should be out in a year. I guess you can go buy it."

"Well, maybe you could bring me a copy before then."

"Oh it won't be out for another year, ya know, so, yeah," William replied as he bit his knuckle and looked away.

She walked closer to him and put her hands on his shoulder and looked directly at him with worry in her sparkling blue eyes. William knew this was not the conversation she had been expecting. He wanted to look the other way and fake it, but her glow would get the best of him. It was hard to make a split second decision, but if he just stood there she would know he was drunk.

145

"But you're gonna be around to see it though, riiiight?" She pleaded.

"Ahh no," He softly replied under his breath. "Anyway, maybe we should get started."

Once again he didn't know why he choose her to spill the story to her. A moment of anxiety came to him as he realized he may regret this tomorrow. He hoped that she really did care about him and did not think of him as just another doucebag customer she could make money off of.

"William, you don't need some sexual arousal, you need some real love and caring."

"Yeah, well, I didn't get any love or caring. Besides, it doesn't matter."

"Of course it matters," Cherry pleaded.

"Why? I'll do better in the next life, I swear. In this life I resisted all temptation to kill anyone. Unlike my past life, I think I did good this time and won't need constant punishment like I got in this life."

"You think you were bad in the past life?"

"Well, something has been wrong. I've just been under a constant curse my whole life. Part of the reason I'm done is I now know I'll never be able to break the curse. It will always be like this. No matter how I try I cannot break free."

"You know believing you're cursed is what makes you cursed."

"I know, but it's just too much, too many bad things happened and I just see a circle, it's just round and round. I'll do better in the next life, I swear. I wont let them get to me."

"What if there is no next time? Why are you doing this?"

"I hope there is a next life so I can try again. I guess I'm doing this because I became what I used to laugh at and hate. I mean as a kid I would laugh at guys who would visit some burlesque house or strip club. I thought they were pathetic to think those girls cared about them. I remember at the diner when I first started when I was sixteen these guys would come in and talk about how the girls at the strip club really actually liked them. I always laughed and would say under my breath 'they like your money' and it was true. I never though I'd be like that."

"There's nothing wrong with it, William. Tons of guys come here.

That's not a reason to shoot yourself."

"Yeah, but, after my war with the Casners I hated rich fucks who buy off the city officials to get away with murder basically. That's me, only I'm far from rich. I became my worst enemy. Even if Roger did cheat I only got the record back cause I bribed the track coach. Then I set the kid up to be arrested for something he didn't do just like the Casners did to me."

"Ya know this Roger kid sounds like he was on a path to destruction. It would've only been a matter of time before he got arrested," Cherry said.

"I know, but I let some shyster con man come in and totally destroy my relationship. If I could go back in time fourteen years and go to the diner and have the young me wait on me now and chat with him, he would think I'm a complete loser. I don't know how it happened. I fought and fought for years. My old girlfriend was shot to death right in front of me.

"This time it's not about winning some personal war, it's that I'm done. I won my wars, but for what? So I could slop food at a diner and live in house on the diner property?"

The two of them spent too much time chatting that they didn't have time to do any of the things they normally do. When session was over, he didn't mind losing out on his fantasies. He was glad to chat with her. She grabbed his hand as they walked toward the front door, something she had never done before. She gripped it hard as they walked down they hall. They reached the metal front door and she unlocked it. Right before he made it through the door she stopped him.

"William," she said in distressed tone. "I don't wanna talk about it here, but we're gonna talk about this." William continued to walk through the open slotted metal door. She shut it and locked it but through the slots he could see she was visibly disturbed. Making her upset was not his intention. Although she was not mad at him he didn't feel like she deserved anymore stress than she had to. He stood on the other side of the locked door and looked at her more.

"I've been there myself, William," She added before she left the foyer to go back to the rooms. He went to his car and drove away. His mind was so fixated on what just happened he forgot to blink for a while. It was wise of him to keep his eye on the road with the amount of alcohol still in his body. He meticulously stopped at every stop sign fully and never went under or above the speed limit.

The next morning he woke up with a headache.

"Oh shit! What did I do last night?" he said to himself.

Throughout the day he kept thinking he should go back after work and tell her it was not true, or it was a prank or something. Then he would change his mind and be glad someone knew of his plans. That night he went back with his mind set on telling her that he made it all up and was so very sorry.

"Oh, you're back. I didn't know if I'd ever see you again," Cherry said as she answered the door

"Well, I wasn't like gonna do something last night. I mean I said I was gonna wait," William replied as they went to a private room.

"You really had me freaked out last night, William."

"Yeah, I wanted to talk to you about that. I was just drunk and made the whole thing up."

Cherry gave William "the look."

Once again her charisma won him over. Instead of saying what he intended to say, he broke down and admitted the truth. She just seemed so open to wanna talk about his troubles. It was like no matter what he said she would never use it against him or throw it back in his face. He knew that he was too uncomfortable to talk to Mitch and Riley about this and that Andrea and Shelly didn't care. She sat next to him with her arm around his body.

"I don't think you were making it up," Cherry said.

"Well, you're right, but it's not like I could just do it right away, I got too many unsolved problems," William said.

"Like?"

"Who do I leave all my stuff to? Nobody fits all my criteria."

"What's your criteria?"

"Well, I wanna leave my stuff to someone who A, deserves it. Someone who has done good for me and helped me in any way they could, a person who stood up for me when things were rough. B, I want it to have an impact on their life. I mean I want it to be what like sets them free and totally changes their life. C, It has to be someone who will make it grow, not just flush it down the toilet."

"Nobody meets that criteria?"

"Okay, I told you about my boy Mitch. He deserves it. It would have a huge impact on his life, but he doesn't know anything about food or business and will just end up running it into the ground. Same with Geoff, he's never run a restaurant he wouldn't know what to do. Riley does deserve it and would know how to run it, but it wouldn't set him free. He's an engineer. He doesn't want to spend his life slopping food at a diner. He would probably just sell it for dime on the dollar."

"Well, maybe he could use the money from selling it?"

"Unless you find the right buyer who really wants it, you're basically selling the equipment. He wouldn't get shit for it. They only way to make money is to keep it going, not sell it at bottom dollar."

"I understand what you mean. A diner is something most people wouldn't even want. What about your ex's sister with the kids? I bet the kids would like to have a place to live."

"Okay, Shelly could sure use the house part for her kids. It would set her free and she would grow off of it, but, she basically pledged her allegiance to Ralph. It's tough to know what to do. I hate to think all my hard work would just go to shit."

"Well then, you'll just have to stick around and keep the diner for yourself," Cheery pleaded.

"I don't want to. I've had enough. Besides, my next life is gonna be so much better. Think of the possibilities. I might end up as anything. Hell, what if I ended up being someone with endless possibilities like the Casners were? Every day I waste in this life is one I could've been putting towards the next one. If I had done this fourteen years ago when I was found guilty in court I'd be like thirteen years old now. Why waste time in a lost life? I wanna put it all for next time. I know it will be better."

"How are you sure of that?"

"Because I swear I won't let them get me next time. I won't let people like the Casners fight with me like they did. I won't let my relationships be sabotaged by con men. I wont let it happen, they won't get me next time."

"When are you planning to do this?"

149

"I'd say like August, maybe like the 1st. Ya know, less than month or so, time is running out."

"Don't exit now, William. You don't have to," Cherry pleaded.

"I want to."

"Okay, look our time is up, but I want to meet up with you outside of here before you do this."

"You do?" William said, confused.

"Yes, I do. Does Wednesday work for you?"

"I'll make it work. I'm shocked. I figured you didn't care. Thought I'd ended up like one of those guys I used to wait on and was just deluding myself that you really liked me."

"Why wouldn't I like you? You think cause I work here I have no feelings at all?" Cherry wondered.

"I figured you must have some filthy rich husband who looks like a movie star and is perfect in every way. You probably live in a big mansion and guys like me serve you drinks."

"Yeah, nice try. The last guy I dated was as useful as a mosquito on a horse's ass."

"Oh really?" William laughed.

"There you go. First time I've seen you smile. You wanna meet at your diner?"

"Oh, hell no! We wouldn't get a moment's peace. There's this place near downtown called The Vineyard that I thought we'd try out."

"Okay, I'll meet you there at 4." Cherry replied.

The two of them left the room and headed toward the front door.

"I better give you my number, just in case something happens," William said. He passed her a slip of paper.

"Do you want me to call you?"

"Texting's probably better. It's hard to talk while I'm working."

"Okay. You're not gonna do anything stupid before then, right?"

"No. I am so happy to be able to hang out with you on the outside."

"The outside? Are we in prison?" Cherry replied as she unlocked the metal front door to let William out.

"Kinda, in a way we are prisoners."

"You're funny. Goodnight William."

"Goodnight, Cherry."

"Actually, my name's Christina."

"Oh good. I was gonna say that was mean of your parents to name you Cherry."

Chapter 12

Dinner Date

After closing time on the night before the big date William began his usual drinking pattern at the bar. This time he drank out of bliss that he would get to see Christina for a real date the next day.

Tonight he decided to walk around the closed diner and reminisce about the past. All the memories of being fired over and over and fighting with the Casners when he was eighteen made him shake his head. He felt saddened when he remembered eating there with Annie and Andrea.

"Those days are long gone," He said to himself with a drink in his hand. William wanted to think the next day would be the start of a new future. He almost believed it.

The next day William approached Riley.

"I got something very important to do, can you run the place for a while?"

"Sure. Where are you going?"

"That's a secret."

"Oh, you and your damn secrets."

For the first time in a while William made it somewhere on time. Inside the restaurant the hostess crossed off his reservation and led him to his table. It seamed like a dream that he was actually here with a girl he met at The Love House.

The fine atmosphere of the restaurant was exactly what he wanted for afternoon. Reprints of fine artwork and newspaper clipping that featured the place were on the walls. He laughed when he saw that The Vineyard had a certificate that showed they donated money to the New Laws program.

"Oh boy, it's five after. Is she gonna show?" William said to himself.

He bit his knuckle and then played with the salt and pepper shakers. He got up to look in the parking lot, but didn't see Christina's Land Rover. He went to the bathroom to wash up and walked around the restaurant. Finally he sat back down. Even though she was only ten minutes late, it seemed like much longer.

"You made it," William said as she came up to the table. Even though she looked different on the outside than she did in the club, she still had the same sparkling energy. William laughed to himself at how much different she looked fully clothed. She sat down next to him and didn't hesitate to get close and personal.

"Yes, I did. Did you think I would stand you up?"

"I had hoped you wouldn't."

They started off with salads and two orders of Tanqueray and tonic. Before diving into the deep conversation they did a toast with their drinks and ordered their main course. By the time the food arrived they were on their second round of drinks. William started off about why he wrote the book and his plan to exit early in life.

"I heard what I'm gonna do is a sin. Do you think God will be mad at me?" William asked.

"He just might."

"Well, maybe I can explain it to him. Besides I'd like to have a chat with him and ask him why he gave me so many terrible challenges in this life. I wish I could've had a charmed life like a lot of other people do."

"I don't think God has to explain anything to you. If anything, I think it's you that would have to explain why you left when you still had so much to do. You don't exit because a few bad things happened. You're supposed to fix it. That's the point of being alive."

"Ya know, Christina, it's not just about becoming like the Casners or Andrea leaving me for some dipshit. It's that my glory days are over. Last night all I did was walk around the diner and remember good times."

"Your glory days haven't even started."

"I've heard that. Maybe it's true, but I don't feel any hope."

"You really don't want to fix it? I mean after all the things you said you've been through, why quit now? It seems like it's not nearly as bad now as it used to be for you."

"No it isn't, but I had more hope and spunk then. I thought if I beat the Casners that everything would be just fine forever. I though that's all I had to do in life was beat them."

"Well, we're ignorant as kids. There's sure a lot more to do in life than just beat your enemy."

"You got that right. I dunno. It's just that back then all I cared about was my car and having fun. I had nothing to lose and everything was fresh and magical. Even just going to the mall was a magical experience when you're eighteen. The only reason I needed money was to keep the Lincoln going and have fun with friends. Owning a business and thinking of more than just the end of the week sucks."

"Um, from what you told me you were like the most hated man in town and in a world of shit when you were in school."

"I think I was miserable, but there was just a good feeling I had then. It was like I felt alive, like everything was always okay." He said as he dredged up the past.

"What do you mean, honey? How can you say it was all good? You were on your way to prison and expelled from school," She said with puppy dog eyes.

"It's hard to explain. There was something about not caring or knowing about the rest of your life, I just lived just for the day. I didn't even know what fourteen years was. I remember thinking that it was kinda cool to just live in noble poverty and be persecuted."

"Yes, there might be something fun about being reckless, but you can't just live forever in childhood. I'm sure you were quite scared when you got arrested at eighteen." Christina replied.

"You know, this is weird, but when I got arrested seemed like a fun experience. It sucked, but it was my first tour of the jail, a new fresh experience. Also I had a delusion that I was some big time criminal that the authors of the world would want to write about. The memory of being on front page twice was devastating, yet it did make me an infamous celebrity. At one time everyone in town was talking about me over drinks or dinner. It was like everything I did mattered."

"Oh, William. I would bet you if we could go back in time your younger self would not be telling me how fun it was to be in jail," Christina said with love in her eyes.

"I don't know. Maybe if you went back, I would be crying in your arms about having to go to jail. I remember it being kinda cool and exciting. I didn't have so much going on back then. Life was simple and it was my first time around the block. These days I just can't get the same feeling I once did from simple pleasures.

"Going to the mall is just a chore on my list of things to do in a day, not an immense experience. The memory of being young and thinking I could do anything keeps coming back, but I don't feel that way anymore. I keep asking myself if this is all there is. Am I going to slop food at the dinner till I'm as old as Lois? The days of thinking I would be a world famous athlete or movie star are long faded. Every year I have to cross something else off my list of things I may get to do.

"In my heart I wouldn't mind if Roger beat the track record, but another part of me would be sad that the one decent thing I did in my youth will fade to black."

"In some ways that's good," Christina replied. "The good thing about getting older is you don't have to be a movie star to feel like you're worth anything."

"Yeah, I guess it doesn't matter as much that I never really made it big. I just don't want to be like my old boss Lois. She worked her whole life at the diner, and for what? She paid off her crappy house with the money I gave her and gets to go on a little cruise. That's it. You work your whole life for one tiny little crumb? She's gonna get old and probably have to sell the house and go to an old folks home. Within a few years her entire net worth will be sucked up to zero."

"Maybe she felt she had a full life. Know how many people don't even end up with that at the end?"

"I know. You're right. I'm giving up early and not even for the best reasons. Things really aren't that bad, I'm just sick of it all. Honestly, I just postponed it to have dinner with you."

"Well, I'm glad you're alive." She replied with a smile.

"Today I am, too," William replied, still immersed in thoughts of the times of yore.

"You're not gonna have those thoughts anymore are you?"

Christina pleaded.

"Probably, unless my glory days return again."

"You know, your mind plays tricks on you. I learned about it in this psychology class I took. Many people have mid-life crises because they only remember the good times then and the bad things now. If you could go back to your supposed glory days for even a week you would probably be happier in the now than then."

"I don't know. I dealt with things better back then. I didn't care about my future. I just did things without a thought of consequence. It was stupid, but it was fun. Even the country was better. Everything was better."

Christina laughed. "At least once a month my grandfather calls me talking about how we need to get America back to the good ol' days. You know, the way it was when he was a kid when everyone was honest and worked hard and people cared about each other. It doesn't matter that he was growing up during the holocaust. Nor does it matter that his father was saying the same thing. All grandpa knows is that he can remember a time when everything was wonderful."

"Yeah, that's a good point."

"There is the famous video where you are told to count how many times a ball is passed around. A gorilla walks past in the background and you don't even notice cause you're watching the ball."

"I've heard of that. What does it prove?"

"That when we focus on just one thing, we miss everything else. I would bet you money that in another twenty years, and I really want you to live another twenty years, you will be saying the same thing. You'll be saying that everything was so easy and wonderful when you bought the diner. These will be what you end up calling your glory days."

"Hmm, I didn't think of that. What else did you learn?"

"That we can convince ourselves that things that didn't happen actually did. In class I got to be part of this experiment. There was this guy in the class that I'd know for years. I went to his mom and got some old pictures of him from his sixth birthday party. Me and some others did a Photoshop on them to show he got a new BB gun for his birthday.

"I told him that his mother gave me the old pictures of him from when he got a BB gun for his birthday. After he looked at the picture, all of a sudden he remembered getting the gun and how much he loved it. He started going on about memories playing with it.

"The problem with our mind is that it is incredibly easy to manipulate. By skewing a certain stimulus, say the photo, you can trick the brain into thinking that it is remembering something that didn't happen, as long as it is similar to something that could've happened. Or, even better, if it seems like it should've happened. In your mind you think that high school years are supposed to be the best years of your life, so you are remembering them as such. I would love to go back in time and ask you at eighteen if you felt these were the best days of your life."

"Really? Oh my God!" William said almost choking on his drink.

"Yep, the same can apply to you. I bet Roger right now feels his life is garbage, especially since he may go to jail. It wouldn't surprise me if in fourteen years he was like you and saying that being arrested at the diner with cops chasing him was such a cool experience."

"Wow. You are a lot smarter than I thought."

"Oh, did you think I was some dumb blond bitch?" Christina said half sarcastic.

"No, but, you know..."

"I work at The Love House, so I can probably only do sexual things, right?"

"No, you're an angel."

"William, I had thought about doing the same thing, but I didn't."

"What stopped you?"

"I don't know. It's just human instinct to want to survive. It was close. I just had kinda the same things, no family support, loser boyfriends, crap jobs... I just wanted out."

"You just reconsidered, huh?"

"Yeah. It wasn't some big epiphany, I just didn't do it."

"Was it worth it? You glad you didn't?"

"Yes. I learned to deal with it better. Also, figuring out what I just told you helped. I don't sit around dreaming of my great youth. I remember that it sucked."

"Why? Didn't you have any good times? Didn't you feel the same freedom, freshness in life?"

"Yes, I had some good times. I'm just not gonna get sucked into remembering some great life that might not have even be real. You're not the only one who does this, hun. Tons of guys that come to club tell me all about when they were young and all the parties they went to and the women they fucked and drugs and booze 'n stuff. That's what their mind chooses to remember. Their mind doesn't remember how bad they felt the morning after partying too much or the women that rejected them or going to jail or being beat up."

"I get it. I wish I could say I feel better, but I've just had enough and it's really getting tough?"

"You gotta fix it. You don't have to exit yet," Christina said with a smile.

They finished their dinners and took a moment from dark conversation to enjoy the ambiance of the restaurant. Lucky for them the place was slow and they didn't have to worry about their conversation being overheard. After another round of drinks they decided to order dessert of mud pie with Oreo cookies on it

He took in every word she said and really tried to think of bad times when he was young to see if he was just remembering what was good then and bad now. He even realized that if he did live another decade he may only remember having dinner with her and forget all the days of moping around he had done. Although she made him feel better, he wasn't ready to abandon his plan.

"You know William, you said you hate it that you've become like the Casners."

"Yep, I'm William Casner now."

"What if you changed that? Did something the Casners never did? What could you do differently now that you're in their position?"

"All they ever wanted to do was break my chops and have me put away. A few times they sure came close."

"Well then do something completely different with this Roger kid. Do something that is totally out of character of what happened to you."

"We tried to tell him to train hard and try again in September, but he just smokes pot and gets in trouble."

"He might not be self motivated like you are. Maybe he needs someone to train him and inspire him."

William's tilted his head. "I'll have to think about that."

After everything was finished, William paid the entire tab and they left. In the parking lot they hugged and smiled at each other. He wished this moment could last forever, but eventually she pulled away.

"Do this again?" William asked.

"Well, I'm busy for a while, but come August I'll have lots of free time."

"Yeah, maybe in August we can do this again."

"You'll have to stay alive 'til then, you know."

"Yeah, I know," William replied as they bid farewell to each other.

The next morning a blissful William woke up and made a phone call to the District Attorney's office. His frustration rose as he was transferred three times before getting the right lawyer on the phone. A memory of when the town was more simple and the D.A. could be reached directly came upon him as he waited on hold. He tried not to let that thought turn into another "glory days' thought. Finally, the lady he was waiting for answered.

"This is Janet Cellars," she said in a pleasant tone.

"Hi, Ms. Cellars. This is William Defreno. I wanna ask a favor of you."

"What's that?"

"The case against Roger Delahoy, I want to drop the charges."

"It's a little late for that."

"I know, but I really want to do this. can you make it happen?"

"William, is Roger making you do this?"

"Oh come on, if I didn't let the Casners bully me I'm sure not gonna let that dufus do it."

"Why do you wanna drop the charges? Is Roger intimidating you?"

"That little bag of bones? Hell, no! I just want to cut the kid a break. I'm sorry to waste everyone's time."

"Okay." She sounded frustrated. "You need to come down and see me in person and sign a few things."

"I'm on the way."

Chapter 13

Meet the New Boss

That night at the diner William felt much better. Since profits had been high the last few weeks he was able to pay Riley a hefty bonus for pretty much running the place alone. Although he found it necessary drink while he worked, he felt decent. After an early evening rush the place slowed down as the sun set on this long summer day. William looked out the front window and saw just what he was hoping to see, Roger Delahoy outside the place smoking pot.

"What'cha doing here?" William asked as he went outside.

"I was trying to get enough guts to come inside and ask you why you dropped the charges against me."

"A poor boy like you could use a break."

"Well, thank you. I won't bug you anymore. I'm gonna crawl in a hole and die somewhere."

"Hold on," William replied.

"What?"

"Before you crawl away forever, I gotta know right now. Did you cheat the track coach?"

"Duh, of course."

"Why?"

"Man, I wasn't trying to take your record. I was just trying to get out of running that last lap. Then all of a sudden it was this big deal.

"So if you didn't want the record, why didn't you just come clean?

"I couldn't. Everyone was making this big deal out of it. For the first time people noticed me. Guys wanted to sit with me at lunch. The girls were actually talking to me for like the first time ever. I couldn't give that up. It just felt so good to finally have some sort of accomplishment. I'm not good at nothin'. I mean you were a natural, you were just born running fast. I wasn't born good at anything. The only way I'll ever get anything in life is to cheat or steal it"

"First of all, I wasn't a natural. Yeah, I had some ability, but I didn't just go out one day and decide to beat a track record. I trained my ass off to make it happen. I worked for it."

"Some of us don't have that luxury. We gotta take what we can get."

"But wouldn't you have to know that you didn't really break the record?"

"Yeah, but I figured I'd get over it and convince myself I really did run it that fast. I'm lost in America, got nothing to do and even less to lose. So I guess I wanted to be good at being annoying and an outlaw."

"Man, all you can think of doing with your life is cheating and being an outlaw? Didn't that New Laws program teach you anything?"

"Oh man, fuck those cock munchers!"

"I pay lots of money to them. They swear up and down their tough tactics really work on troubled kids. They try really hard to give kids like you an alternative to crime and a meaning in life."

"They came to my school in May. They certainly swear up and down alright. My little cousin Charlie is in the 6th grade and had to go to summer school. Those dickweeds are coming to his school to harass everyone."

"Well, statistically kids who have to go to summer school are more likely to have criminal problems. They're just trying to help your cousin not end up in jail."

"You know what? Since you donate so much to these fools, maybe you should go to the school and see these guys first hand."

"Maybe I will."

"If you do, tell 'em Roger Delahoy said they're a bunch of ass pirates," Roger replied as he took a drag off his joint.

"Gimmie that," William said as he snatched the joint out of Roger's mouth.

"What do care?"

"Because track stars don't smoke weed."

"I ain't no track star."

"No, not yet, but yer gonna be."

"What'cha mean?"

"I mean tomorrow you show up here at 5 P.M. with some decent running shoes and not reeking of smoke."

"Are you crazy?"

"I think I'm beyond that. In forty days school starts. If you man up and do what you need to do, you can beat that track record by then."

"I can't beat shit."

"Okay, how about this, if you don't break that track record I'm gonna beat the shit outta you again," William said with sarcasm in his voice.

"What do you mean again? If the damn law hadn't showed up, you'd'a been toast that night," Roger replied.

"Uh huh, this is just what a girl I know was talking about. You are only remembering what you want to. You didn't stand a chance that night. Those cops saved you a whole lot of healing."

"Okay, fine. I'll get some running shoes and be here tomorrow."

As promised, Roger showed up at the diner at 5 P.M. with a new pair of running shoes. The shiny new shoes looked good. William was pleased.

"Asics, nice choice," William said.

"Thanks. Man, I could've bought a whole lot of weed for what these things cost."

"Yeah, well life sucks sometimes. Speaking of that, here's seven dollars. Jog down to the store and get me some Lucky Strikes."

"What? I thought track stars didn't smoke."

"They don't, and when I was one I didn't either. But, that was fourteen years and two titanium pins ago. Now go. And don't stop running till you get there."

"Okay," Roger said as he began to run.

Before long he returned. As promised, he didn't stop once on the way there or on the way back. William smiled as he took the cigarettes out of Roger's shaking hand. Roger began to cough up mucus from his lungs.

"Well, there's your weed," William said.

"What?"

"I'd say you just hacked up about an ounce of weed from your lungs there."

"Oh man, that gas station is far."

"Yeah, it's about one third of a mile, so both ways you did two thirds of a mile."

"Oh crap, that's really far."

"Yep. Now I want you to practice this thing called horse stance. You pretend you're sitting in a chair and squat down until your legs are parallel to the ground. Take a piece of broom handle and balance it on your legs. If it rolls off your not down low enough, if it rolls toward you you're too low."

"Holy balls, this hurts!" Roger blurted out after getting into the stance.

"That's the point. Your legs should feel like they're on fire. That's how you know you're doing it right."

Roger tried over and over to last ten seconds in the stance but struggled. Because of the pain. He also kept coughing up more junk from his lungs.

"This blows," he said as he retched yet again.

"Hey Roger. After not smoking a full day and running hard the cilia in your lungs will work better cleaning them out."

"What?"

What I mean is your body has healing to do and the detox process isn't gonna be fun."

"How bad is it gonna be?"

"You will get headaches and dizzy feelings. You may sleep a lot and maybe even see stars. But it should go away in a few weeks and you will feel better."

"Oh man, that sucks."

"I know, but that's the way it is. Same time tomorrow. No smoking tonight and drink a protein shake when you get home and lots and lots of water."

"Agreed."

Over the next week Roger showed up every day and jogged to get William something from the gas station. He would bring back everything from gum, to cigarettes to candy. They would do more leg muscle building exercising and strategic stretching. No matter how hard he tried, Roger couldn't hold the full horse stance for longer than a few seconds.

"Okay go into the stance and when you can't take it anymore then stand up," William said.

Roger did it again and stood up after only thirteen seconds.

"Okay, you stood up after thirteen seconds because your legs couldn't take it anymore, right?" William asked.

"Yeah man, they were done."

"Got some bad news for you, the few seconds it takes to stand up is harder than staying in the stance. If your legs were truly shot, you would just fall over, you wouldn't be able to stand. It's your mind that gave up, not your body. When you're down there you have to be in control. When your legs are burning you have be say to them 'can't help you right now.' On the last lap when you retest your mind is going to want to give in. You have to learn now how be strong enough to push it when you think you've had enough."

"Oh man, it's rough."

"Let's try again."

After another week, the thirteen seconds made it up to fifty five seconds. While doing the stance again, William noticed Roger seemed to be on the verge of tears.

"What's the matter?" William asked.

"My body has just been feeling so weird. I hate it."

"Oh, that's the smoking withdrawal again. When you replace sitting around smoking pot all days with running, vitamins and protein shakes, that's what happens." "I would never be able to make it though this without you William."

"Oh geez, stop, or you're gonna make me cry, too. Like were in some A.A. meeting or something."

"Oh yeah, speaking of meetings, today your New Laws buddies are going to my cousins school."

"Yeah, I know. They said I could get a school pass to watch them in action if I wanted."

"You said you would, man."

"I know. They'll be there after lunch at like one according to the website."

"I can't wait to see what you think of them afterward."

"Actually, it turns out I can't go," William stated.

"What! Come on, man! You promised!"

"Naa, forget it."

"What do you want, man?"

"Hold horse stance for me for one full minute and I'll go," William replied with a smile.

"You son of a-"

Roger went into the stance and the stopwatch began. After thirty seconds the pain was horrible, but he continued to hold. He gritted his teeth but did not stand up or move.

"Come on Roger, twenty more seconds."

"I can't do it."

"This is how you are gonna feel on your last lap when you test. You have to be able to hold it. The last lap is harder than the first three put together."

"Okay, Okay," Roger squeaked out.

"Fifty seven, fifty eight, fifty nine, one minute, you did it," William said.

Roger fell to the ground. It was true. His legs were so tired he couldn't stand up and had to fall over. After a few moments of his legs coming back to life, a virtuous feeling came to him as he had held it for as long as needed. Roger got up and danced around to get the full feeling back. William wondered if this was the first time he ever accomplished anything.

"Okay, I'm gonna go to the school and check out the program. While I'm gone you're gonna jog one mile with these one pound dumbbells strapped to your legs."

"Why do that?"

"If you train to run it with weights, it will be easy the day you can do it without them."

"Okay."

"Jog to the gas station and back and to the station again as fast as you can. Then walk back the second time to cool down. Then."

"Okay, I got a shake left."

"Actually, get some good protein today. When your done go

inside the dinner and tell Riley to get you a big steak on the house."

"Really? you know how longs it's been since I got to eat steak?"

"How long?"

"Since the last time the butcher turned his back long enough to not see me take one."

"I'm gonna pretend I didn't hear that."

"Yeah, yeah, have fun at the school listening to dumb and dumber."

"I'm gonna tell those guys about you stealing that steak," William joked.

Chapter 14

New Laws

At a little before one, William arrived at the middle school where kids from all over had to do summer school. The receptionist checked his I.D. and showed him which classroom the New Laws program was doing their presentation in.

"It's Ms. Banks classroom," The receptionist said.

"I don't know her. What's she like?" William replied.

"Well heads up, she has the most loving tenderness for her students. She turned down a higher paying job in medicine to teach. But, everyone knows not to mess with her. She has zero tolerance for nonsense."

"Ah. Thanks for the warning."

William walked down the hall and entered the classroom and saw Ms. Banks teaching math. He waited till she was ready to acknowledge him and felt nervous that he was disrupting her class.

This confident, well educated black woman was both physically and mentally strong. She wore classic woman's business attire and had a beauty salon hair style. William could see she did not seek the approval of anyone including himself.

"May I help you?" She asked.

"Hi, I'm here to watch the New Laws speech," William said.

"Go ahead and have a seat, they will be here shortly."

William tried to sit in one of the students desks but it was clear he was too big for it. His attempt to try to squeeze into it slightly disrupted the class. It seemed weird to him to sit on the floor or stand. Ms. Banks silently pointed at her desk in the back of the room. He sat down in the comfortable office chair on wheels and waited for the speakers to show up.

"Okay children," Ms Banks said. "I told you these police officers who go to all the schools are coming today to do a demonstration for you. They're activists in keeping crime down and young teens from being troubled. I want you to pay attention and give them your utmost respect."

William could see the kids had the utmost respect for her as they all said "yes ma'am." William leaned back in the chair and put his feet on the desk like he did in his office at the diner. Before Mrs. Banks noticed he took them off the desk and had to remind himself he wasn't the boss around here. Like the kids in the room, he also wanted to be as respectful to her as possible.

Three guys walked into the classroom. Two of them were wearing their blue police uniform and hat but not their police duty belts that would normally have had their gun, cuffs and weapons on it. Both of them were tall, white, clean shaven and looked like brothers. They must have been from back east with their bright wrinkled Irish faces. William laughed to himself because they looked like pigs.

The third man was a short black guy with corduroy pants, dress shirt and bow tie. His short buzzed hair and intellectual eye glasses screamed "total nerd". They came to the front of the room and prepared their speech to the kids. Ms. Banks sat down at her other desk in the front of the room. William was excited that he was a large donor to this program and hoped they lived up to their great reputation.

"Hello," the nerd said. "I'm Booker, these are my co-workers Mike and Ike. We created and promote a program called New Laws." His soft and overly proper tone of voice only added to his image.

"That's right," Ike said in a rough and loud tone that matched his appearance.

"Oh yeah, you got that right." Mike agreed in his identical rough eastern accent.

"Kids," Mike started. "The reason we call it New Laws is because in the last year there have been many new laws passed to help with the growing crime problems. Huh, huh, New Laws!" he barked.

"Yes," Booker said. "The state lawmakers, in conjunction with community leaders, have passed some new laws that will help to bring to a standstill some of the growing crimes," he continued in his proper tone.

"Yeah, yeah," Ike said. "What Booker's tryin' to say is yer no longer gonna get away with it anymore. Tell 'em Booker."

"Okay," Booker started. "The first new revised statute pertains to shoplifting. This could be as simple as stealing candy from the store."

"Yeah, I'm sure all you little brats have stolen something from the store," Mike added.

"Shoplifting used to be punishable by up to thirty days in jail," Booker said.

"Yeah, no wonder it happened so much, thirty days isn't gonna stop any of you from doing it. How much time can we give 'em now? How much time?" Mike said, excited about the increase in punishment.

"Now that same crime is to be punished by sixty days."

"Uh," Mike said. "That still ain't enough. Did you mean sixty weeks?"

"Nope, sixty days." Booker stated.

"Well," Ike said. "That sure isn't gonna stop anything."

"Okay," Booker continued. "The next new revised statute pertains to the sale of controlled substances. This would include the sale of marijuana, heroin, cocaine, methamphetamine and crack cocaine. Under the old law such a crime was to be punished by up five years in prison."

"Yeah," Mike interrupted. "But not no more. We gotta new law for that!"

"Yes we do," Booker continued. "Now such offenses can be punished up to eight years in prison, depending on the amount and value of the drug."

"What?" Ike barked. "You know, personally I don't think even that's nearly enough."

"Oh man! Not even close!" Mike barked even louder.

"Yep," Booker said. "Now, the penalty goes up if those controlled substances are manufactured. The manufacture of any of those drugs was up to fourteen years, but now can be punished up to eighteen years in prison."

"Oh my God!" Mike said waving his arms. "That's it? Eighteen years? That's nothin'! What the hell?"

"Man," Ike started. "I hope you mean like Mars years, cause a Mars year is like six hundred in something days a year."

"There are six hundred and eighty-six days in a Mars year," Booker added.

"Even that's still not enough!" Mike said. "That ain't gonna stop these kids from makin' meth. I'm thinkin' more like Jupiter, Neptune or Uranus years. Booker how many earth years in a Uranus year?"

"Eighty-four earth years equal one Uranus year," Booker added.

"Oh, hell yeah! Now were talking! Now were gettin' somewhere," Mike said.

"Yeah, that would be a great idea to sentence them in Uranus years," Ike said. "I gotta great slogan even these little idiots could remember: break the law and we'll sentence yer anus in Uranus years," Ike said followed by laughter. Mike also laughed at it as well. Ms. Banks stood up from her desk with a scowl on her face.

"Excuse me officers. Perhaps you gentleman should consider being astronomy teachers instead of police officers. So far, I am not liking this demonstration one bit."

"What, what, what?" Mike replied. "You gonna get mad at me cause I care about this community?"

"Oh, you care about the community?" She snapped at them.

"With all my heart. I've lived here most of my life and I'm tired of these little thugs ruining this place 'cause they don't get no punishment."

"You don't care about this community, you just want to put everyone in jail," She said in displeased tone.

"Could we continue please, Ms. Banks?" Mike rudely replied.

"Please do."

"Good," Mike said. "Alright, Booker, what's next?"

"Alright, there is a new inclination going around called 'the knock-out game'.

Basically, young teens go around and punch someone in the face to try to knock them out for thrills. If you play this game the only thing that will get knocked out is many years of you life."

Mike laughed. "Good one, Booker. The knock-out game. The fuckin' knock-out game. Think about it, Ms. Banks, you could be at yer favorite supermarket gettin' some groceries and one of these little punks come up and tried to knock you out so they can get into some loser gang. It could happen to anyone."

"Almost anyone," Ike added. "I would love it if one of you little morons would try to play the knock-out game on me. Ho, ho, I'll be a pallbearer at yer funeral."

"A closed casket funeral," Mike added.

"Oh yeah, I can see it now. 'Gee Mr. Police Commissioner I don't know how he got thirty seven bullets in him.'"

All three of them laughed. Ms. Banks shook her head. William could see that they had hit rock bottom in her mind. It was not possible for her to have any less respect for them. She intentionally put on her meanest glare as she looked at them. It didn't seem to dampen their wickedness one bit. In fact, they seemed to get louder and more heated with each law they read.

"Alright, Booker, how much time can we give 'em? How much time? How much fuckin' time? How much fuckin' time?" Mike shouted.

"If one plays this game it is to be punished by up to twelve years."

"No way!" Mike said as he grabbed Booker and shook him. "You gotta be kiddin' me!"

"Hold on, hold on" Booker insisted. "If it is determined in a court of law that the assault was part of a gang initiation an additional punishment can be added."

"Okay, great," Mike said and released Booker. "Additional, that's my favorite word when it comes to punishing you little peckerwoods. Additional, additional, additional, I love it. How much additional time can we give 'em?"

"Additionally, another three years can be added if gang involvement was a factor."

"Oh, man- this is- oh you gotta- I'm outta here," Mike said as he walked toward the door.

"Where are you going?" Booker demanded.

"What? It's not enough! It's not enough!" Mike said as he turned around and violently waved his arms in the air.

"Get back here!" Booker said.

"I can't believe you think it's enough, Booker."

"I don't think it is, either."

"Well you sure have a funny way of showing it."

"I'm in better control of my emotions."

"How can you be in control of your emotions? These like dumb fucks are gonna knock-out your mother and get a slap on the wrist!"

"Yeah," Ike added. "Then another slap on the wrist! You think fifteen years is enough for these chuds to stop doing it? I bet every one of them is gonna go out tonight and play it cause they know they'll get away with it."

"Well," Booker said. "How much time do you think is fair?"

"Man," Mike said. "I'd say bare minimum should be twenty-five years. That's if you get down on your knees in court and beg for mercy and if Judge Foster is in a good mood. Like, she just got laid by a super hunk the night before. Twenty-five years of scrubbing Bubba's undies, and that's absolute minimum."

"Oh yeah," Ike replied. "And that don't happen too often. She's sixty-eight years old. She probably smells like salmon. So twenty-five years probably ain't gonna happen too much. I like thirty-five years better."

"Me, too," Mike said. "Let me tell ya, Judge Foster is so nasty she had to get her babies drunk to get 'em to breastfeed off her."

"Ha, ha, ha, that's fucking funny man," Ike replied as Mike came back to the front with the other two.

"Hey Ike, how bout forty-five years?" Mike said.

"Oh my God, now were talking. How bout fifty-five years?"

"Oh yeah, I think I'm gettin' sexually excited. Down boy," Mike said to in pants in reference to getting an erection. "I'd love to see any of you fools get that much time," he continued.

"You know what," Ike said. "I bet every one of these little imbeciles has broken at least one of these laws. Come on you little hoodlums, how many have you broken?"

A thirteen year old caucasian student named Joe started to sob. William had noticed the kid had been on the verge of tears. William could tell both Mike and Ike wore it like a badge of honor that they made a student cry.

"I stole Snickers from the Circle K. I'm sorry, I don't wanna go to jail," Joe said and continued to shed tears.

Ms. Banks went over to comfort and assure him he would not have to go to jail for stealing the candy bar. A thirteen year old black student named Darnel who had a small thick afro with a comb stuck in it for style and a large plastic alarm clock around his neck started to giggle. His giggle then turned into hard laughter. He even pounded the desk for dramatic effect. As Mike approached him, his laughter only got louder and louder.

"Somethin' humorous there, half-wit?" Mike asked.

"Yeah, you! You guys are stupid!"

"Oh really?" Mike said as he got closer to Darnel.

"Yeah, you guys remind me of monkeys at the zoo," Darnel said and continued to cackle at them.

"Ya know," Mike replied. "Speaking of crimes, last night I was on patrol and the Guitarland was burglarized. Some crook got away with a two thousand dollar Fender guitar. The description we got was a white male in his thirties with long gray hair who rode off on a high performance motorcycle."

"So?" Darnel replied.

"So, I'd say the description fits you perfectly. Where's the guitar you little delinquent?"

"Man, I have a rock solid alibi for last night," Darnel said with a laugh.

"Oh yeah, where the hell were ya?"

"I was with your wife all night while you were workin'. Man she could suck a golf ball through a garden hose."

"Oh, you little mother- son of a freaking- Goddamn punk ass!" Mike bellowed as he went toward Darnel. Both Ike and Booker pulled Mike away and towards the door of the classroom. Even with both of them it was hard to restrain the fuming Mike. They each grabbed one of his arms and proceeded to escort him out. Mike fought with hard resistance.

"Come on, guys," Mike yelled. "Gimme five minutes alone with him! Just five minutes!" They continued to pull him toward the door kicking and screaming.

"Come on, Mike. We're getting you outta here," Booker insisted as he pushed him out the door.

173

"No, no. Just gimme one minute, that's all I need. I'm gonna whip yer ass you little son of a bitch!"

They got him out to the hallway and the classroom door shut. Loud, unintelligible roaring could be heard from the hallway even with the door to the classroom shut. After a while Booker came back in with his glasses knocked a little crooked. He kept his composure as he went back to the front of the classroom. He got his notes organized and was ready to continue.

"Alright, children, I'd like to finish our--"

"Just thirty seconds that's all I need," Mike boldly interrupted as he barged back in the room.

"He got free!" Ike said as he chased after Mike. Booker helped Ike restrain him again.

"Come on, just ten seconds, that's all."

Once again they took him out to the hall. This time Booker stayed out there with them till Mike calmed down. Inside the classroom Darnel was still chuckling to himself. Ms Banks had to get an aspirin from the desk William was sitting at.

"You know," Ms. Banks said to William. "I thought earlier that they had hit rock bottom on the amount of respect I had for them. After this incident they somehow penetrated the rock floor and sunk even lower."

William just smiled and nodded as she threw the pill in her mouth and washed it down with water. She returned to her front desk.

"Man, I wish school was this much fun every day, I'd never ditch again," Darnel said.

"Zip it, Darnel," Ms Banks commanded. He obeyed.

The three of them came back in the classroom with a calmed down Mike. Darnel gave Mike a quick grin that nobody else saw. Mike pointed at him and then to the ground to say in sign language 'you're going down.' Booker made sure no other outbursts were going to happen before he proceeded. They finished their presentation within the next ten minutes and asked if anyone had any questions.

"I have one?" Ms. Banks said.

"Yeah?" Mike said.

"What exactly in your sick minds does this do to prevent crime?"

"It makes these little bastards think about their behavior. Next time their sittin' around their hood maybe they'll say 'yo man, they ain't messin' around with us no more, we best behave ourselves.'"

"You know these kids are like twelve and thirteen?" Ms. Banks pointed out.

"Hey, you can never snip a weed too young. You been breaking my balls the whole presentation. Why is that?"

"Yeah, well I'm not a big believer in your hard core, three strikes, you're out, lock em' up and throw away the key tactics."

"Hey," Ike interrupted. "I in no way believe in the three strikes law. I don't in any way think if someone get three felonies they should automatically be put in prison forever."

"What?" Mike replied. "I'm a huge believer in it! You're not?"

"No, Mike, not at all. Why is it you think these little hooligans should be able to victimize three innocent people? Why can't we get 'em the first time?" Ike replied as he threw his hand up with one finger raised to emphasize first time.

"Ha, ha, you're right, Ike! You've totally changed my view. I no longer believe in the three strike law. You've shown me the light. I hope all you little summer school lowlifes have seen the light today, too. This concludes our program."

"Okay, that's what I thought," Ms. Banks replied. "Since you're done, would you please get out of my sight?"

They left and prepared themselves for the next classroom. Ms. Banks spoke to the kids about the presentation. This was not at all what she thought the program would be like.

William left the classroom and walked toward the front entrance of the school. He passed by the next classroom that was getting the presentation. He could hear Mike screaming the words, "it's not enough, it's not enough," even through the walls. He continued to walk out until he reached his car. Roger was there waiting for him.

"What are you doing here?" William asked.

"I jogged down here."

"Really? That's like three miles."

"I know. I only took a break twice the whole way. I can't believe it."

"Good job."

"How was New Laws?'"

"Yeah, great, they really care," William replied. "About what, I have no idea."

"Yeah, they suck big time. Maybe if they want kids to stay out of jail they should do what you do and give them opportunity to achieve a goal."

"Yeah, I suppose so."

At that moment William realized he was not like his old rivals the Casners. It seemed like he actually might have saved Roger from being put in the system at a young age. The refreshing feeling made him a little misty eyed. Now more than ever he wanted Roger to win the record. If only Christina could be here to see this. He realized it had been over a week since he saw her.

"Well, you're on a roll and never slowing down. Might as well jog back. I'll see you at the diner."

"I bet I get there first," Roger said sarcastically.

Chapter 15

Time Is Running Out

By August 1st William had trained Roger to run the mile in just under five minutes. While outside in the warm air his cell phone rang. Due to bad reception outside the call rang once and went to voicemail. He looked and saw whoever called him blocked their number. After he sent Roger to the store for an ice cream bar he checked the voicemail.

Message one: "Hi Honey it's Christina. I know you were planning something bad today, but I really hope you changed your mind and that you're okay. I'll try you back later."

William realized he had no way of contacting her and the last few times he went to the club he had missed her. The only way to make sure he didn't miss the call was to stay close to the diner because reception was better there. When Roger came back with the ice cream bar he let Roger keep it and made him do more horse stance. For hours he gripped the phone to make sure he didn't miss the next call.

William went inside to use the bathroom. The diner phone rang.

"Moe's Diner, this is William," he answered.

"Hi, William this is Rachael, I'm a friend of Christina's."

"Oh hi, how are you?"

"Good. I was thinking of coming to the diner tonight with my husband. Can I make a reservation?"

"Sure. What time?"

"Oh, like seven."

"I got you down for seven."

"Great. Thank you. Bye."

William went back to training and gave Roger a water break as they both went back inside the diner. Riley was getting a bit overwhelmed so William and Roger helped catch him up. After the lunch shift, Roger, William and Riley sat down for steak and shrimp lunches. William smoked a little more than usual because of the call from Christina. Although Roger didn't usually eat much he forced down the steak for the protein as William had advised.

"So how goes it? Is he a track star yet?" Riley asked.

"Close," Roger replied. "I can do a mile and a half without stopping."

"Yeah," William added. "Also I noticed you've stopped hacking up every second of the day. Your lungs are probably done with the initial detox."

"Wow. What's it been, like three weeks?"

"Yeah," Roger said. "I hardly even feel like having any smokes."

"Good," Riley replied. "Keep it that way even if you don't break the record. Don't be like William here smoking his life away."

The diner phone rang. The number showed it was Christina's friend again.

"Moe's Diner," William answered.

"Hey, sorry to do this, but we can't make it tonight, so we need to cancel our reservation."

"Okay, that's fine. Come see me another day."

After they hung up he wondered why she called only to cancel later. It seemed like it was planned. The best theory was that Christina had her call him to make sure he wasn't dead. The three finished their nice lunches and William and Riley prepared for dinner shift. One of the waiters had finally done a no-call, no-show for the third day in a row. Under the diner policy that automatically resulted in his termination.

"Roger," William said.

"Yeah,?"

"Wanna wait tables tonight?"

"Okay."

"Get outta those sweaty ass clothes and get these slacks and white dress shirt on."

William knew this was Roger's first job. Even though Roger had never waited tables before he found it came easily to him. To

William's surprise a cleaned up and detoxed Roger looked pretty professional. After a busy evening Roger's mouth dropped at the amount of tips he made in one night.

After the diner shut William began his usual drinking at the empty bar. He smiled as he thought of Roger's progress. He felt relieved that instead of destroying the kid he was building him up. Before long he had consumed more drinks than usual. He debated whether to have more drinks, or if he had enough.

"It's not enough, it's not enough," he said to himself, stating that he had not drank enough yet. After a few more he decided to go see if Christina was working tonight. When he arrived her automobile was in the parking lot. A wave a delightful came upon him. He had missed her the last couple times. After the check-in process it was not long before she came in the private room.

"Glad you're here," she said.

"Yeah, I've been training that Roger kid hard to beat my record."

"Oh, you're helping him, huh?"

"Yep. I don't care about my old record. I want him to break it."

"I knew you were nothing like the Casners."

"He gets to retest September 3rd at lunchtime."

"That's great! I'm proud of you."

"How about you? How are things around here?"

"They got new management around here." Christina made a face.

"Oh, how's that going?"

"Well, let's just say we don't exactly see eye-to-eye, but I'll be ok. You will let me know if he wins?"

"Well, yeah."

William spoke with her a little longer before she gave him a nice massage with their time that remained. The good feeling that radiated off her still had not faded even thought he felt better. When time was up he left and didn't realize that he still had no way of communicating with her besides the club. She did have his number, but he didn't have hers. The thought of his bed was a superb feeling after all the alcohol wore off.

With one week to go until the big test, the detoxification of his lungs and body greatly improved Roger's stamina. The money saved by not buying pot along with a job at the diner allowed him to buy all the nutritional supplements he could.

Yet, he was still struggling with speed. Beating 4:50 legitimately was a challenge William didn't know if Roger could actually meet. Today they worked short hundred yard runs. Even though Rogers's shoes felt like they were on fire, he kept running.

"Man, Roger, you got to be able to pick up the speed in the middle. You start out fast then slow down, then fast again. It's got to be constant," William stated.

"I know. The middle is always the hardest. That's why the middle child gets screwed."

"Oh? Enlighten me."

"You remember the first day of school, the last day of school but who remembers the middle day, the halfway point?"

"Yeah, that makes sense. You the middle child?"

"Yep. I didn't get all the hype of being the first and didn't get to be the spoiled one like the last. The middle sucks."

"Okay, back to running. Every part is important. You gotta push it just as hard in the middle as the end. When you think you got nothing left, think of a credit card," William said as he pulled out his Visa.

"Credit card?"

"Uh-huh. You're gonna borrow some energy and stamina. Just picture yourself swiping that card until your levels are recharged. Like the card, you'll have to pay it back later when the test is over."

"That's pointless and stupid."

"Yeah, well so is giving up your favorite bad habits, spending your summer training and then not breaking the record."

"I know. I gave up my girlfriend for this," Roger said with a hint of cynicism in his voice.

"Who was yer girlfriend?"

"Mary from Tijuana."

"Mary from Tijuana? Oh wait, I get it, Marijuana. You little wise guy. Just like the broken track record and 'The Long Run'."

"I'm sure you were a wise ass, too. What was this town like when you were eighteen?"

"Oh, Roger, totally different. It was dictated by evil emperors Randy and Carol Casner. In every supermarket there were red rugs that would hang from the ceiling with their picture on it in a green suit."

"Yuck."

"Oh, that's not all. There was this twenty foot tall brick wall that went around the city proper. Guards would dump hot oil on anyone who tried to escape. All this was run by Randy and Carol."

"I kinda heard what happened. They were busted."

"Yep, and I'm the one who brought down their empire. They had the cops in their pocket and city council under their thumb. There was this huge bronze statue of them downtown, but I pulled it over to symbolize their fall of power."

"I kinda saw what they looked liked in the papers."

"Well, pictures you saw were when they took off the helmet. They used to wear these big black helmets and their voices were computerized."

"Did they have lightsabers?"

"Not quite, just a cell phone they would speed dial 9-1-1 when they saw me driving around. When they die, they're gonna find all the old cops on their payroll and bury them alive in their tomb. That way they can serve them in the afterlife."

"Seriously man, how did you do it by yourself?"

"I had some help from Mitch and Riley. I don't know. It's like this track record, when you break it you're gonna wonder how you were able to do it. You just do it. You never give up."

"Wow, not only did you crush the dark emperor, but yer gonna help me beat your own track record. That's really great of you. You should get a place in the city's history books."

"Yeah, we'll see. I think I already have one," William replied.

Chapter 16

In the Long Run

With just days to go before the big test both William and Roger were getting anxious and edgy. William was glad the day was coming up so he could be done with it no matter how it turned out.

That night before the test after everything was done at the diner William decided to go see Christina because he had missed her the last three times. He arrived in the parking lot and didn't see her car again. This time he rang the doorbell to see when she'd be back.

"Hi, honey. I'm Destiny. Who are you?" A young attractive girl said as she answered the door.

"Hi, I've been wanting to see Cherry for a while, but I keep missing her."

"Cherry got fired about two weeks ago."

"What, why?" William wondered.

"Don't know. The boss just let her go."

"Oh man," William said in bottomless sorrow.

"Hey, whatever she does for you I can do better."

William felt so struck down by Christina being gone he didn't want to just go home. He decided to go with Destiny to ease the melancholy of Christina's disappearance. They sat down and she asked what he wanted to do. He explained the things that him and Christina would do when they first met.

Destiny did a grand job of performing the same acts and scenarios and Christina. She was extremely attractive with her smooth bright face, long brown hair and overly cumbersome chest for her thin body. She giggled and was as nice as she could be to William. She must have been twenty years younger than Christina as well. William smiled and enjoyed the stay. But, it seemed that trying to replace Christina would not be something that could happen.

"Was that fun?" Destiny asked.

"Yeah, it was," William replied as he realized he didn't want to break her heart and tell her she just didn't have what he needed. After he left the club a good feeling came upon him. He now knew for sure that it wasn't just Christina's looks that made him hanker after her. He figured that most guys would think Destiny was younger, thinner, and more energetic and had a nicer chest. It was truly something about Christina that made him glad to be alive.

His next thought was negative. Christina was gone. He had no way of knowing where she was or what she was doing. Although she may have had his phone number, he doubted that she would ever call him again. His head hung low and grief and hurt is all he felt. When he got back to the diner he drank too much again. The only positive thought was that Roger needed him to finish what they'd begun.

William woke the next morning ready to do what he needed to do for Roger. At noon both William and Roger showed up to meet Mr. Perez.

"Roger, you ready for this?" Mr. Perez asked.

"Yes."

"Okay, so that we don't have confusion like last time, I have four flags. Every time you do a lap I will throw one to the ground. When you see the last flag in my hand you will know you are one lap from being done. I will start the stop watch when I say go. Both feet must cross the finish line before I will stop the watch. Do you understand these rules?"

"Yes."

"Did you stretch out?"

"Yes, all morning."

"Okay then, get ready to go," Mr. Perez said.

"Alright Roger," William said. "This is it. Just make it happen. Use everything you got. Borrow energy if you need to. Don't stop 'til you hit that finish line."

"You got it, man. I'm ready."

"On your mark! Get set! Go," Mr. Perez said as he started the stop watch.

"Go, go, go," William yelled as Roger completed his first lap.

"What's his time so far?" William asked.

"1:25."

"Oh boy," William said. Roger needed to do each lap in 1:17 or less. The first lap is supposed to be the easiest because you're fresh and full of energy. The second lap was even worse with a total time of 2:40. William was already preparing what to say to make Roger feel better about not breaking the record.

"Look Roger, I know you're disappointed, but getting in shape is never a waste of time," William said to himself in rehearsal.

"3:32. One more lap to go," Mr. Perez said.

William glimpsed at Roger, who had picked up the pace tremendously. That time 3:32 stung like a bee. He knew it had significance to him but didn't know exactly why at the moment. Roger was halfway done with the last lap with the stop watch at 4:00.

"Come on, Roger! Do it! Run!" William shouted at Roger who looked like he was in considerable agony.

"Come on! Run like hell! Ruuuun, dammit, run! Run, run, run!" William bellowed at the top of his lungs with his hands waving in the air.

"Come on! Do it! Do it!" He continued.

A hammered Roger crossed the finish line. The pure adrenalin he had wore off in a microsecond. Roger fell to the ground and even scraped his face as he rolled to a halt. Mr. Perez and William heard Roger coughing up acids and whimpering in pain and woe. William went over to check on him while Mr. Perez stood with his eyebrows raised and jaw slightly dropped.

"He's alive. He'll be fine," William said to Mr. Perez.

William checked the stopwatch in Mr. Perez's hand. He grabbed a gallon of bottled water and went back to see if Roger was doing any better. Roger was on the ground, on his back with his tongue hanging out for effect. With his lungs panting and face bloodied, he couldn't grasp enough air to ask the results. William dumped the gallon of water on him to cool down his body and wash away the dirt from the tumble and roll on the ground. Finally he was able to sit up, but not stand.

"Can I declare bankruptcy?" Roger asked.

"What?"

"I mean I borrowed so much energy I'll never be able to pay it back. I wanna settle on it or something."

"Wise ass."

"Yeah, I know, Hold on." Roger said as hacked up more gunk and clinched his cramping stomach."

"You know, Roger, it's better to lose fairly than it is to win cheating. Last time when you cheated you got 4:41 to my 4:50."

"I didn't get 4:41 this time?"

"You didn't."

"Piss," Roger replied coughing some more and wiping the wet gravel off his bleeding face. He tried to stand up but his legs didn't work.

"Oh man, I felt like I was floating that last lap. I mean I couldn't even feel my legs."

"Yeah, that's the right feeling. That's how I knew you were cheating last time. You hardly made it seem like it was anything."

"Yeah, well if I'd gotten away with cheating I'd have it."

"Yeah, you'd have it at 4:41."

"Oh well, I had a fun summer at the diner at least."

"Well, before we break out the tissues, you didn't get 4:41, you got 4:39. You did better fairly than you did cheating."

"No way."

"Yep, congrats. My old faded plaque has been up the fourteen years, but today it comes down."

"Wow, what do you think it's been doing all those years?"

"I don't know, Roger, collecting dust probably."

"Do you think it gets bored and lonely? Maybe tired of sitting up there all those years?" Roger wondered.

"Dude, what've you been smokin?"

"The track record, that's what I been smokin."

"Very good," William replied as he helped Roger up. The three of them walked to the gym to take down William's record. Mr. Perez used a large machine to engrave the new plaque for Roger. William shed a tear as he remembered them taking down Randy Casner's plaque to put his up fourteen years ago. Now there was nothing left at the high school that bared his name or memory to it.

"I'm gonna keep this and hang it up at the diner," William said as Mr. Perez finished Roger's plaque and handed William his old one.

When they put the new plaque up William was startled to see that it said:

"Roger Delahoy

1 Mile Run

Time 4:39

Trained by predecessor William Defreno"

"What?" William said.

"Well," Mr. Perez said. "I've never seen such good sportsmanship. I think it's only fair you stay recognized as an important member of the track record memory."

William walked with Roger to what was left of the day's classes. As they walked in the hall they heard some obnoxious yelling coming from the auditorium where many students and faculty were gathered for freshman orientation. Both Roger and William peaked in and saw three familiar guys on the stage.

"That's it? Ten measly years for a crime like that? Booker this is bullshit! It's not enough, it's not enough," Mike said. William and Roger just laughed and went on their way to Roger's class.

"Thanks William, I would've never done it without you."

"Just keep it going and remember this can be a great thing for your life, but don't think it's everything. Study in school, stay off the weed and obey the new laws."

"Yeah, it wouldn't have mattered how much jail time they gave me. I would have been a hoodlum anyway. Now, I wanna do good. Maybe next year I'll break it again to make it impossible for anyone else."

"That's the spirit," William replied as he watched Roger go to class. He stood and watched for a moment with a smile on his face. His mind slipped into delusion for a moment as he could see an image of his young self walking the hallways after beating the track record. The young William image gave the older William a thumbs up and a smile. Luckily, he was in the hall alone or someone would've thought he was a screwball as he smiled at an imaginary image.

After the big day was over it was time to head back to the diner.

Although victory had been achieved, it seemed sad not to have to train Roger between shifts anymore. Also Roger would be working fewer hours now that school had started. All night, William thought of the day he broke the record and the terrible consequences for doing so. Every event that happened to him started from the day he broke the record.

"What would've happened if I never broke that record?" William asked Riley at the bar.

"I don't know. The war with the Casners would not have happened. They might never have been busted for their crimes. Roger would never have broken it. Funny, the world would be a different place for a lot of us if you had not broken the record."

"Annie would not have been killed," William added with a cheerless voice.

"Yeah, well who knows. If I ever go back in time I'll break you're legs so that you can't beat the record."

"Then I'll just fight with you," William added.

"Yeah, well it's funny how an event can change so much. Who knows maybe it would've been worse for you. Nobody can ever know."

"Yeah, well I'll bet Roger's gonna sleep well tonight."

"Man, he's gonna be sore tomorrow. Hey, look, William a new customer, wanna wait on her?"

"Yeah okay." William agreed as he approached the solo customer waiting to be seated.

"Hello, welcome to Moe's Diner can I----oh my God!" William said as he saw it was Christina.

"Hey there," she replied.

"Hi, uh, you're here to see me, right?"

"Of course, silly."

They sat down at a booth. At first he was silent because he didn't want to let her know right away that he was in the process of grieving the loss of her. Riley brought them artichoke dip for an appetizer and gave them menus.

"What brings you here? I thought you were fired and gone," William asked.

"Oh, I was, but it's okay. I was ready for a change anyway."

"What are you going to do now?"

"Well, I only need like twenty credits to finish my degree. Thought I might go back to school, maybe become a student counselor or something."

"You would be awesome at that," William exclaimed. He could imagine her prying dark secrets out of troubled high school students. They'd confess as easily as he had.

"Thanks." She reached for her glass of water. "Did Roger break your record?"

"Yep, 4:39. That's even faster than he got cheating."

"Good to hear. All your training did well."

"Yeah, I guess I did something successfully."

"You do lots of things successfully, William."

"You mean like tonight? You know I carried an antenna all the way to the top of the Sears tower earlier today. Man, that thing was heavy!"

Christina laughed and William joined her. Although the wreckage of the past haunted him, the belief that one day he really could "live happily ever after", or at least close didn't desert him. An endless loop of thoughts went through his head. Would this be the end of the wars? Would he finally find someone to share the dream with? Would the diner really make it big? He would have to find out in the long run.

DID YOU ENJOY THIS BOOK?

SEND QUESTIONS OR COMMENTS TO THE AUTHOR:

DAVE AQUINO
P.O. BOX 741351
ARVADA, CO 80006-1351

Books by Dave Aquino

Personal War

Personal War Part 2

Personal War Part 3

Counselor

The Slot Machine

www.ingramcontent.com/pod-product-compliance
Lightning Source LLC
Chambersburg PA
CBHW020436180626
46812CB00003B/1269